D1357083

90710 000 504 619

HOW
TO
GUT
A
FISH

HOW TO GUT A FISH

SHEILA ARMSTRONG

BLOOMSBURY PUBLISHING
LONDON • OXFORD • NEW YORK • NEW DELHI • SYDNEY

BLOOMSBURY PUBLISHING
Bloomsbury Publishing Plc
50 Bedford Square, London, WC1B 3DP, UK
29 Earlsfort Terrace, Dublin 2, Ireland

BLOOMSBURY, BLOOMSBURY PUBLISHING and the Diana logo are
trademarks of Bloomsbury Publishing Plc

First published in Great Britain 2022

'dado' first appeared in *Fish Anthology 2020* (Fish Publishing) and 'lemons' in
Best European Fiction 2019 (Dalkey Archive Press)

ISBN: HB: 978-1-5266-3577-8; TPB: 978-1-5266-3581-5;
EBOOK: 978-1-5266-3579-2; EPDF: 978-1-5266-4680-4

2 4 6 8 10 9 7 5 3 1

Typeset by Integra Software Services Pvt. Ltd.
Printed and bound in Great Britain by CPI Group (UK) Ltd, Croydon CR0 4YY

To find out more about our authors and books visit www.bloomsbury.com
and sign up for our newsletters

Contents

hole

The weakness in the soil first appears at dusk in the centre of a ring of stones in a field. A small copse of trees weaves around banks of raised earth, and the exposed roots of a yew tree frame the slabs of an ancient portal tomb.

The field belongs to a farmer who believes this corner does not really belong to him at all, and he prefers to leave the fairy fort well enough alone. He takes care to follow the well-worn route of his cattle closely as they pass through the field; he avoids it at night because the grass is hungry and may not let him leave.

Whitethorn blooms here in summer, and in autumn, circles of mushrooms sprout in brown formation. But this year, the winter has been so wet that the rain has been constant, and the level of the water table has risen far enough to press its head against the roof of the earth, kneading and marking like a gentle tide. Layers of soil have fallen away from the weakness in between the stones, setting more layers in motion.

how to gut a fish

Above the field, the December light streaks off into the red horizon, and the horizon after that. Grass plinks as the longest night of the year begins.

The centre of the stones darkens, and the collapse of the topsoil into a deep sinkhole comes all in a sunset rush. The air trembles like a bent sheet of tin.

A stone wall separates a green-spined boreen from the field and the concrete sags in the middle, like an under-baked cake. The road has flooded from the heavy rain, two-metres wide and a handspan deep. The puddle has frosted over the past few nights, but the temperature has risen a little from the bitter depths of November, so at twilight it teeters on the edge of freezing.

A steering wheel vibrates as a car barrels through the deep water, but the windows are fully closed so the driver hardly notices the splash. This shortcut home from the Christmas party in the Parish Hall is handy for him; it makes a fifteen-minute journey out of a five, so it is a long-cut, really. But there is no chance of a checkpoint after his few glasses of mulled wine, so he can press the accelerator to the floor without disturbing another soul, except for the two donkeys, who are used to drunken stragglers leaning in to stroke their broad noses and occasionally curling up in their lay-by until dawn.

hole

In the crepuscular light, a hare slinks out from the copse of trees and over the wall; another follows it, and another. The three hares leap to the centre of the road, turning to stare, unconcerned, down the barrel of the headlights.

The driver has lamped for rabbits and foxes before, hanging out the window with a near-gale roaring in his ears to mask the car's approach, the red beam of torchlight circling the field. He knows how the eyes of small things shine golden under the beam; knows the stunning of the light. But the three animals face the swiftly approaching car, ears back and noses high, not dazzled nor frightened a tick.

The man considers driving over them for a moment – just a moment – then brakes, hard. One of the hares jiggles its head from side to side like it is trying to shake its own ears off. All three turn in unison and bound back across the belly of the wall. The driver slowly switches off his engine, opens the car door and steps out to follow them into the field.

The evening is greyscaled, but the hares' eyes are copper holes.

———

Full darkness comes early in December; the moon is round and pale in the sky. The afternoon was sullen under low, damp clouds, but the banks have cleared and now the night is almost as bright as the day.

how to gut a fish

Two fourteen-year-olds dawdle down the lane. Neither wanted to be the one to suggest coming here, so after the cinema, they instead meandered around the outskirts of the town for an hour, kissing in corners, playing Would You Rather and coming up with more and more depraved choices. Now, the excuse of a full bladder has finally brought them to the fairy fort.

The girl leans over the wall and hikes up her jeans before stepping into careful toeholds in the crumbling rock. The boy raises an arm to help but she doesn't look back at him, hopping from the top of the wall to the grass in one great leap. She disappears to wee against the dark silhouette of the yew tree.

The boy calls to her, then again, louder. He begins to shiver in his duffel coat, uneasy among the gentle noises of night. A cat was found burned and hanging by its tail from a tree here last summer. The rumoured cat-killer is in their secondary school; he slouches around town with one hand in his pocket and touches himself outside the newsagent's.

Other grisly myths drift from the stones like pollen – changeling children, ghostly hounds, joint-eaters that will follow you home – but bent beer cans still litter the ground because the spot is sheltered enough for a campfire, and a hard, flat slab known as The Mattress is infamous in the school locker rooms.

hole

The girl pops out from behind the yew tree and the boy presses his hand to his forehead and sways, pretending to faint in surprise. She smiles at him, a slow and wild smile, and her hair lifts away from her face in a sudden shifting of air. The night inhales again and she seems to come to a decision.

The girl's heavy jumper rises up a little as she turns towards the fairy fort, her pierced bellybutton a dark hole that swallows the moonlight. The boy opens his mouth to call out and tastes the iron pull in the air. He begins to climb after her, so fast the skin of his palms splits red on the rough stone wall.

Hours of silence, and the trees exhale. Coppice stools line the boreen, trunks sliced off at the base with long fingers of bark curved and turned back down into the soil; an army of dead spiders. The new shoots are thin and spindly, and the farmer plans to harvest the hazel in a couple of years for his fireplace, if the trees allow it.

A female badger snuffles her way around the stools and begins to root uneasily at the edges of the new hole for grubs. Excavations are familiar to her; she has begun to dig a new sett out of an old sett beneath the yew tree, uncovering the skull of a distant cousin who died under a collapsing roof of soil. But there is something unwelcome in the air tonight.

how to gut a fish

The badger sow begins to walk in slow, widening circles around the sinkhole, moving her snout from right, to down, to left, to down again, her paws causing the faintest of tremors. The soil is sharp against her underbelly, pockmarked by cattle hooves, and the grass has frozen in white, downy patches.

After a while, a badger boar emerges from the hedges and attempts to mount her as she circles past him. She tosses him away with a twist of her hindquarters, then leads him back under the cover of the brambles. The pile of scree outside the new sett is small, but it will not grow further; the appearance of the hole has unsettled her, and she will find a better place to birth her young.

In the sky, constellations rise and set around the sink of the moon.

———

After midnight, a man on a bicycle turns down the boreen on his way home. His mood is dark: there had been an argument in the pub, or something shorter and lighter than an argument; a local barfly had called him The Great Defector and hummed a few lines of a song.

The man is used to this after three years in Ireland, and worse, but his date was annoyed on his behalf, and made him talk for an hour about his parents and six-year-old son back in South Korea. She drank red wine and seemed disappointed that he had only sipped his second pint of Guinness and waved good-bye to her instead of kissing her on the cheek.

But his son's mother has arranged a video call from Seoul in an hour; his boy is anxious about a new teacher at school and needs coaxing out the door in the morning. The man hates the sight of his ex-wife, hates the shiny screen of his laptop, hates the distance of his own son; he sometimes wills the screen to break so he can reach through the portal and pull the boy across the continents and into his own arms.

The moonlight catches the surface of the flood-puddle like glass and he veers into the field to avoid it, into a narrow ridge where bicycles have taken the same path over weeks of detours. His wheels stutter on the uneven ground and he feels the bike veering away from him, leaning in towards the fairy fort. The tyres skid on the wet soil and lose contact – a long, stretched-out moment where he is flying, and his skull feels as light and fragile as a wet sheet of paper – and then the mooring line of his son pulls taut and the bike finds an equilibrium again.

He barks out a laugh, and another, and another, until he is speeding away down the lane, away from the ring of stones, howling his reprieve to the moon. *Alive, alive, alive*, he pants in time with each down-stroke of the pedals.

A nighthawk comes around four in the morning with his metal detector. He is convinced that ancient treasures are waiting just under the soil of the barrows: twisted golden torcs, bronze arrowheads, the wide cup of an engraved goblet.

The man who sold him the machine told him the law is hazy – *you can find, but don't look* – and winked like the wealthy villain in a cartoon. It's not that he's afraid of being discovered, exactly, he tells his wife, he just prefers to come searching at night; it's easier to hear the soft beeping of the metal detector that way. She is always asleep when he leaves, or pretending to be, which suits him. His wife is having an affair with a younger woman in her office, but he finds only relief in it. Her softening body doesn't interest him any more, if it ever did, and to his mind they are welcome to each other – the night and its treasures are his alone.

A headtorch sways on his forehead as he shivers in the cold December air, surveying the thin blanket of ownership that hovers just above the soil. He opens an amateur archaeology app on his phone and scrolls with a dirt-stained thumb for any new entries. Red arrows dig into the map on his screen, discoveries marked by other nighthawks. Descriptions pop up under his fingers, a sentence or paragraph, or just a single word – metal, wood, bone.

hole

In the dark, the stone mounds of the fairy fort are almost invisible, but the man purposely parked his car on the main road a kilometre away to allow his eyes time to adjust. He sees the new cavity in the centre of the earthen rings and circles it curiously; a tongue probing the gap left by a missing tooth.

The coil of the metal detector passes over the sink-hole without complaint, and the nighthawk tries again, and again, willing a coin, a bottlecap – anything – into existence. There is a sudden, strong beeping and his sternum leaps like a salmon; he gasps inwards, a dry, sharp noise that is trapped in his throat. He swings the coil back around over the hole again, but the screen only registers two points at his feet: the steel capping of his own boots.

His pulse subsides as he feels the earth shift beneath him, land echoing sea.

A carload of foragers appears before first light, hungover from a winter solstice party that had lasted until two in the morning. Dawn is the best time for mushrooms, the host of the party had announced over gin cocktails; because summer stretched late and the winter has been wet and soft, wood blewits and velvet shanks will be sprouting, and other, more magical types too, if they can find them. Her friends were sceptical until she suggested a foraging party to prove it, and she had sulked on the balcony with a cigarette until they agreed.

The three women and two men step out of the car in silence and stretch as the darkness begins the shift from black to slate grey. They share early-morning tea from a flask and talk softly, as if they are watching a final, private theatre rehearsal before a big opening night. Thin slivers of gauze drape the trees, and the mist is tight and painful in their lungs.

The mushroom expert pulls her silver hair into a ponytail, then sets off across the wall, stumbling a little in the hoof-marked soil. The others stretch again and move, away from the cattle's trail and into the virgin grass, spreading out like the prongs of a rake.

One man in tall rubber boots waits by the car to light a thick joint and watches their figures bend and straighten, bend and straighten. He knows the car journey back into town will be filled with the semeny stink of mushrooms, and he hopes his unsettled stomach can hold out until he fills it with a rasher sandwich at the café.

The grey-haired woman looks back at him as he smokes, and he sticks both thumbs up at her to signal that everything is A-OK. A quirk of genetics has given him thumbs that curve too far around, so that the tip of each one is pointing back towards his own face.

hole

As the sky continues to soften into shades of sepia, the noise of a tractor huffing awake startles a flock of starlings into flight and they perform a swooping murmuration. The birds fold over and back into themselves; a pulsing cloud of magnetic filings.

The sound of the engine travels across the field and the foragers look up, guiltily, but the farmer is used to strange people with notepads gathering around the old portal tomb; *on their own heads be it*, he thinks.

When the tractor passes the car parked on the laneway, the farmer raises his hand in greeting and they return the gesture. The tractor pulls into a lay-by to let a minibus pass. The bus is full of yawning camogie players, on the way to a quarter-final in the city and already nauseous from the early waking. One girl presses her forehead low against the damp window to wave at the farmer, but his eyes are on the field. The girl instead watches as a man in knee-high boots tosses something to the ground and climbs over the wall, around a patch of weeds and towards the fallen stones. She turns to point the man out to the girl in the seat beside her, but her friend has fallen asleep.

Above the bus, the black flock of birds shape-shifts against the sky.

how to gut a fish

Dawn, and the sun stands still just under the horizon, before the Earth begins its long tilt back towards it. The longest night has passed.

The forager wanders, looking for somewhere to sit until the earth stops rolling in waves. He steps around a bed of nettles and comes to the earthen banks of the old fairy fort.

He sees the hole: a green iris of grass surrounding a dark pupil, its edges shaded in gradients from burnt harvest to dusky peat. The rumbling of the passing bus causes the soil in the centre of the stones not to collapse further but to reverse; slowly rebuilding itself, the sides of the hole growing closer together.

He takes a step forward, and another, more urgent, as the opening begins to close more quickly. The grass prickles and clinks as it thaws in the fresh light, and the moisture drips over the shrinking rim, down the umbilical, and deep into the earth.

He stands on the very edge, and his boots begin to sink.

how to gut a fish

1. First, the feel of the salt in the red ridges around your fingernails. The burnt itch of it, the dried white flakes scattered across the empty deck of your father's boat. Now, take the handle of your knife and turn it around. Set the blade back-to-back with the spine of the mackerel and *scrape*. A thousand eyelids will come off, a hundred insect skins, a rainbow of purple and blue and green. Rub, rub, rub until the skin is smooth, or at least smoother – no need to fuss, you'll never get them all, no matter how you try. Your father once told you that if you swallowed a scale, a fish would take seed in your belly and grow.

2. Now, blunt your arms into instruments, and blunt your heart to the little mouth's gasping. Don't forget that stressed fish taste awful, bitter and tough, so don't delay – kill it quickly. But you know your own soul: if it brought

13

in more bookings, you'd set up a system of slow-motion death on the deck of the *Mola mola*, with complicated waterwheels and staggered buckets and cages for dry-drowning. When you visited the dockside markets at Sakaiminato, you saw a fisherman make a careful cut to a yellowtail's head, take a wire and spike it down the spinal cord. No time for the muscles to flex and stiffen, for panic to turn to bitterness; a little flip of the tail, and then it was done. Mercy disguised as cruelty, a quick and shuddering end. The blood coloured a bowl of water from clear to rose-pink to crimson. *Ike jime*, the Japanese call it, a benediction. You'd like to learn how to kill fish this way, as a party trick, but you know your few remaining five-star reviews would trickle away. The mouths of mothers would turn down at the corners, their noses wrinkled like elephant skin, even as their children fling guts at the seagulls. Better the old way, better to break a fish's spine across the gunnels.

3. Find a prayer as the little death whispers away across the deck and over your shoulders into the sunset. Look your fish in the eye: they say the last thing a man sees is imprinted on his pupil. You check every catch this way for your

own reflection, but there is only a dark hole of fright. You switch your gaze from the fish to the sky as the wind picks up; the cold Atlantic air is splitting into two and streaming around the anchored bow of the *Mola mola*. The stag party you deposited on the island for a camping trip must have felt the first chill of it; their newly lit fire is panicked, unsheltered and dim. An hour ago, when you left them at the pier, you told them where to find kindling in the cove, driftwood forced above the tideline by the storms and kept dry under a net of kelp and oarweed. The young lads – were you ever so young? – have pitched their tents in a rough circle around the fire, and now they scurry up and down the beach after a football like sand-hoppers under an uncoiled rope. Somebody scores between two piles of jumpers, directly into the sunset. The excited call of *go-oo-oo-al!* comes low and faint over the water.

4. The first cut with your knife fails, like you are fighting the skin of a mango. The mackerel's body is hard and tight, determined to hold the insides in and the outsides out. The fish is shrink-wrapped, just like you zipped yourself into your grey wet-skins this morning. Your boots and waders are tight against your body

with the warmth of your sweat. Peel off your windcheater for this part; the summer evening is still plenty warm and it's harder to move smoothly in the firm hug of the material. There is hair on your chest, arms, shoulders; a carpet of fur that turns slick and dark like a wolf when the water sprays up and over the bow. Your little sister's daughter is the same: dark tufts of hair where her eyebrows almost come together. When last you visited, you practised making angry faces together, but she had a natural advantage over you.

5. The point of your knife finally goes in at the inverted vent beneath the lower fin. Now drag it along the belly, opening up the seams of the fish. Red and blue swellings of intestines leak out onto your fingers. A female: you'd pop the roe in your mouth if you didn't know better; you've tried, but the puncture and splurt is too full of salted blood and life. You spat it out in surprise like the rind of an unripe tomato. Roe, row, roe all over the floor of your boat – hah! You must write that one down, add it to your father's collection of wooden novelty signs that still hang in the downstairs cabin: GONE FISHING, MASTER BAITER, EAT SLEEP CAST, KEEPIN' IT REEL.

6. Now shake the red pulp off your fingers; slide it through the bailing holes with the side of your boot. Take a bucket of water to the staining if you must. There is still a trace of vomit on the decks of the *Mola mola*. You warned the stag party when they booked the trip that the waves were bigger outside the bay, but still the lads went to the pub beforehand, and arrived on the pier making bets on whose pints would see the light of day again first. The first hour was fine, but as soon as the cliffs fell away, they began to quiet and turn pale, hugging the gunnels. The groom was the first to empty his stomach over the side, a black flood of stout. But soon, all the boys were crawling across the deck; their foreheads forced down by some magnet in the bilges. They piled into the little cabin, although you told them the horizon was their guy-line and their stomachs would be better attached to it. You dumped them at the island's pier soon after. The vomit they left was thick and porous, but you are used to the smell now, and it doesn't make you retch. Nothing you do tonight will make you retch, you try to convince yourself.

7. You can't keep your thoughts to the task at hand; they keep skipping ahead. Back to it.

Next, remove the gills, spread them out like red courtier fans. Make sure you cut them out at the roots — *leave a stump and they might grow back*, your father used to joke. You imagine the gills billowing into lungs this time, lungs that will steal the air from around you, swell up and flip the world around, until the sky is full of water and the deep, the deep is waiting for you with navy breathlessness and stars that glitter out of reach, no matter how you swim. Around you, the sun is draining away and there are no stars in this night yet, and the fire on the island is a weak spark. The ship you are due to meet will not have lights either, but they will find you, you were told, if the *Mola mola* holds her course.

8. Now pause, and see what you have in your hands. A murder scene, a dismemberment. Grope at the insides and pull away the fibres, the black tube of intestine, the white swell of swim bladder. Use your thumb, because the tip of your index and ring finger are flat-paddled, lost half a lifetime ago in a coming together of ship and pier, a groaning of bone against stone. Long-healed, the stubs are perfect for tickling at your niece's belly, pulling wet bubbles of laughter out of her. When she is grown she will turn away from you, like her mother has

done, but the moments when she faces you are apple-sweet and endless, until they do end, and you are driving away from your sister's house with the memory of her husband's forced smiles and a loaf of banana bread that will sit in the freezer untouched for months.

9. Wash out the fish carcass with the hose on the front deck, and wash yourself. While you are at the bow, haul on your anchor line and feed the thick, wet rope through your fingers to test the drag. Squalls come hard and fast over these mountains; the clouds squat to shit out wind in rabid puffs that swing the compass around like a *ceilí* dancer. West and north and east and south; the weathervane startles easily and craves a slow and careful courtship before settling. You wanted to take the stag party out further, before landing on the island, out to the westerly angling spot at the Tanalacht, for pollack and turbot and dogfish. But these lads were not after trophies; they were content to stay close to shore for the trip, to loop fish-hooks into each other's buoyancy aids and piss beers into the ocean. Out at the Tanalacht, the rocks rise out of the water like knobs on a spine, but the arrangement of depths and shallows make the fish leap on to the line. Once, you caught a porbeagle shark

out there with your father. He told you that if they ever stopped swimming, they would die, but the memory is so faint and fragile you think you might have plucked it from a film instead.

10. Turn the fish's spine towards you, eye the curve of it, the smooth arch of the dorsal fin, and *slice*, just above the backbone. Feel the knife press against your skin as you trim the fins away and scrape them off the gunnels. The fire on the island has grown bright and pulsing; you lent the soon-to-be groom a plastic bottle of petrol *for emergencies* and he didn't understand what you meant. You assume by the height of the flames and the faint sound of cheers that he has figured it out, and hope that they have gathered enough driftwood to last. The six-packs and bottles of Jack Daniel's they wedged under their oxters will not be enough to warm them through the night.

11. Put the clean, gutted fish in the ice box, throw the rest of the gore into the night, then turn your back to it. It is too early yet to look for the dark movement of a ship on the horizon, but your eyes swing from the *Mola mola* out to sea and back again like a metronome. Your stomach begins to rotate in a smooth and

careful waltz to the beats of your heart. This is your first time doing this. This is your last time doing this.

12. Pull out a beer from the six-pack the best man left you; *in case of an emergency of your own,* he winked at you from the pier. The light from your cabin makes a heavy pool of orange on the deck, and the opening is covered with a thin film of warmth from the oil heaters below. The island is a darker blot against the night. Shouts of laughter still carry on the breeze; coo-calls of teasing and the roar of drinking games. Come morning you'll meet the lads on the pier, hungover and sand-washed with their tents under their arms. The sensible ones will dive into the cove before they board, drowning last night's fear in the icy bite of the water. You'll come back another day to clean up, to pick through their leavings, to kick sand over the shit that they staggered away from the campfire to do; it will have seemed so far to them in the darkness but by day they will see the closeness of their leavings.

13. Another hour dug out of the night, and your fingers need work to keep them from checking your phone. You finish your beer and

open another, although you promised yourself it would just be one, that your head would stay clear, but your hands have begun to shake. You want to claw your way into the future and have the meeting over with.

14.   You wait in the dark. You wait in the dark.

15.   Your radio crackles to life and your heart is a sounding weight over a deep-sea trench, but there is no message there, just a burst of static. You take out your phone to watch the months-old video of your niece on an Easter egg hunt again. She totters across the lawn to find three chocolate rabbits under a willow tree, and her mouth opens into a great O of surprise. She places them carefully in her wicker basket and jabbers joy at the camera; at you. You turn off your phone and take the steep steps down into the cabin. You check the second, blank phone you have stashed in a pocket at the back of the tiny bathroom door.

16.   While you are below decks, you turn on the gas hob, lighting it with a long, red-handled safety lighter. You hadn't planned on cooking the fish, but the dark waiting is grinding at you. The small hob of the *Mola mola* is used

mostly to make saucepans of tea, black usually, although if you remember you buy a carton of milk and trail it from a line on the transom. The taste of the sea-chilled milk is so sharp and bright you do not want to waste it in tea, but you do, because warm mugs of beige are an elixir on a cold, windy day. *The best cup of tea in the West of Ireland*, one of your reviews said, with a handful of exclamation marks, but your spare mugs have been idle for a full year now.

17. Take the gutted fish from the cooler, and root out the butter, the real butter, that you keep chilled in a lunchbox. Hew a yellow chunk off the block with your knife, crown the back of the fish and wrap some aluminium foil around it, to keep the juices in, to cover the accusing eyes. The cooked meat will melt away from the skeleton, leaving only the silvery colour of mackerel dreams.

18. The heavy, flat-bottomed griddle pan you pull from the cupboard is wide and warms slowly. But you keep it, because your customers used to ask to cook and eat their catch on board, for the real, authentic angling experience. You must have taught a hundred, a thousand of them how to gut a fish over the years, before

the bookings stopped coming in. They would take photos of themselves with their catch and take your details; they'd send you postcards from Alaska, Dubrovnik, Kyoto. You kept the postcards pinned to a corkboard in your cabin until they grew wet and soft around the edges.

19. Your nervous ears have picked up phantoms – a hundred faint hums, a hundred cleared throats – so by the time the real thing appears you are slow to admit it, slow to climb the stairs out of the cabin and into the darkness again. The other ship makes a fleshy, lapping sound in the night, like a dog licking a wound. There is a faded name picked out on the ship's bow in darker red underneath a peeling white stencil. You try to read it then realise it doesn't matter, the name will have changed again by evening to something else. Out of habit you finger your radio and consider hailing the other boat, but you know they will not answer, and you have been warned not to, because the coastguard listens from shore. You know these men are nervous of your nerves, so you try to soften your shoulders.

20. You look at the island so that you don't have to watch the boat coming alongside, the skitter of ropes on your deck. From the throat of

the cabin, the sizzle of mackerel wafts into the sky, the great expanse so full of salt and wet and nothing else to fill it up. The smell would drive a starved man mad. You expect a flock of crazed gulls to descend to tear you to pieces for a taste, just a taste of the white flesh that will separate like threads of thought. But the night stays calm, until the fenders clink softly as the two boats come together.

21. You flinch as the packages land on the deck with a thump so loud you are sure the lads will hear it from the shore, although their fire has banked and almost gone out. If they have fallen asleep outside their tents, they will wake dew-drenched and frozen; the ocean saps the last of the heat in the hollow just before dawn. If tomorrow they speak of seeing a dark shape in the water beside the *Mola mola*, you will tell them old stories about sea turtles and leviathans with a wry twist to your lips. Your father once saw an ocean sunfish and took it for a drowned man; he carried home the sight of the broad, bovine shape spinning ghostly circles in ice-clear water, and named this boat for the memory of it.

22. You begin to count the packages with your eyes and stop, deciding that counting would make

them more solidly there, make the dream less easy to dismiss tomorrow. They form a messy pile, wrapped in black plastic and secured with brown tape. The scent of the fish has turned from a gentle toast to char but you are uneasy, and going below to turn off the hob would mean turning your back on these men with neck warmers that cover their mouths. They confer around you, and, for the first time, one turns to look you directly in the eyes. The fingers on his right hand flick out in a gesture; a blessing.

23. Out of nervousness, you are about to offer the man some mackerel and tea when the metal bar hits your head, and your mouth opens and closes with the shape of the words even as you begin to spill out on the decking. A ringing takes the place of pain, and you look up to the navy sky as the stars begin to drip from the ceiling and the constellations run together into a thumb-smeared windowpane. There is a shuffling of feet and a clunk from the engine that you feel coming up through the deck.

24. The hob, you try to say, you reach an arm up into the air to tell someone to take the pan off the heat, not to waste the fish. The pooling of liquid around you begins to drift through the

limber holes towards the stern. Words fly past above your head; an angry argument about what to do with you. But this is a familiar song, your sister has sung it under her breath for a decade, ever since your father's ashes fell golden on the water out at the Tanalacht. Somebody kicks you, hard, and you are rolled on to your face; your nose is squashed against the deck of the *Mola mola* and electric fire runs from your dented skull down through the plastic and into the ocean.

25. You begin to melt.

26. As the anchor shudders up you silently apologise to the lads on the island and the empty pier they will find in the morning. You think of how the groom spoke about his soon-to-be wife, how the hard parts of him softened and his friends quietened to hear him speak, stuttering, about the place-settings she had personalised, how each table was to reflect a different song from the eras of their lives so far. You wonder how long they will wait on the island for you before ringing the coastguard for help. You wonder if your sister's daughter will wait for you too, stay forever with her eyebrows furrowed in the pretence of anger,

or if her frown will crack and the smile break
over her white teeth like freshwater pearls.

27. You remember the dying fish and you hope
    your eyes will not be full up with fear. You
    hope for a metal wire down your spine, for
    the stiffening and ending of the pain. *Ike jime*,
    you let the clunking syllables fall from your
    mouth as the boat pulls away into the night.
    A benediction.

the skellington dance

A small figure, blurred by the fog of your goggles, comes to the end of the swimming pool to wave at you. You raise your fist and open your fingers wide, twice, to signal that you will do another ten lengths. Your son nods and turns back to his friend Roisín, bending into the beginning of a cannonball.

His shockwave breaks your rhythm, so you switch to a clean breaststroke that divides the water in two; dive and resurface, like you are an eel breaking into the sky. You focus on your breathing as you bring your thumbs together to dive again.

When you were ten, the other girls made a game of running from you. Your dad was a mechanic and drove an old, white van, and they said he was a paedophile, but you didn't know what that meant. He had a brother called Pete you didn't see very often, so you told them *he* wasn't a Peter-file, but your uncle was.

how to gut a fish

They screamed and ran around the schoolyard while you tried to catch up, like pigtailed spiders skittering away from your light.

At a birthday party, somebody's mum had hired a bouncy castle, the first in a flood of inflatables that had plagued that long, hot summer. The girls had laughed and bounced you into a corner, and in your stubbornness you had curled up with your back to them, unwilling to retreat to the safer space of the kitchen, where adults always praised your manners and the thoughtfulness of your gift.

The other girls had begun to climb the sides of the castle – it was old-fashioned, with turrets and crenellations – and the pillars dipped and bowed under their weight. The plastic canopy drooped down and you were trapped under a stretched, multicoloured sky, the air stolen from you on an out-breath. The other children bounced and bounced as you tried to scream them off you, but your mouth was tied up with trying to breathe. The sky, the true sky, appeared in flashes of white as the towers bowed and reinflated in turn. You felt like a flattened, burning tube of paper. You had thought from cartoons that dying would be a quiet, resigned thing, but you hadn't expected the panic, the red awfulness of it.

When somebody's father finally noticed you struggling, his grip around your ankle came through a portal from another world. You cried then, lying on the grass in front of everyone, a great howl of fright, and you didn't know what you were.

––––––

In the changing rooms, Shona and Roisín are already out of the showers. You want to ask Shona if she remembers that party. You think she was one of the bouncing girls, or maybe it was her birthday, but you are afraid she will insist it never happened, that you are remembering it wrong. You quickly hustle Gideon through the showers to catch up to them.

Roisín is shorter than Gideon, even though she is a full year older at eight, and you see Shona surreptitiously hold a towel up as her daughter pulls on clothes. You don't mind, and your son doesn't notice. Art usually takes him swimming, but your husband has a video call this morning, and you aren't yet willing to let Gideon go into the men's changing rooms on his own.

You are already half-dressed, but he is taking an age to dry himself, attacking each limb with the rough shag of the towel. The scar on his back is long and sinuous, bright pink after the shower's heat, and a double row of needlepoints escorts the exquisite straightness of his spine.

You sit at the counter to dry your hair, but the mirrors have steamed up and you cannot see yourself clearly. Your son snaps his new cartoon underwear proudly to show them off to Roisín and you tell him to hurry up.

The lifeguard behind the hygiene screen has tightly curled hair, like an old-fashioned Irish dancer. Her eyes have the red sting of chlorine and the politeness in her voice is tired. But as you leave she winks at Gideon, who had noticed the Pikachu tattoo on her wrist on the way in and stopped to tell her about his collection of Pokémon cards.

Outside, the street is dim and freezing under a low bank of clouds. Your still-wet hair is crisping already, and you haven't brought Gideon's warm hat, but you need to do a shop so you wrap him in your scarf and shuffle him down the road.

Shona and Roisín walk with you for a few minutes; they have ordered their pick-up car for the next street over. Your son is matchstick-slim where Roisín is round and small; Shona jokes that standing together they look like the number ten. Roisín whispers something into Gideon's ear, a giggling secret that is interrupted as the children split to avoid a bleeping smart-post and then resumed on the other side.

---

the skellington dance

When you got sick, eight years ago, you felt guilty, because you thought you had wished it on yourself. You wanted a break; the shop wasn't busier than usual, but you were bored of sorting through lengths of fabric. You watched the red figures roll daily across the news, and the thought of a week in bed seemed almost joyous, a time to catch up on all those series you'd lied about watching.

You had only been with Art for a couple of months when you picked the sickness up, wet and clinging, from a spluttering man on the bus, but still he came by with Lucozade and cough syrup that tasted of strawberry honey. You lay on the couch, complaining that it felt like a fat man was sitting on your chest, and Art pretended to rugby-tackle the shade to the ground. He was the one to call the ambulance in the end, when he found you slumped, breathless, on the floor after a too-hot shower.

Is there any possibility you're pregnant? the ER nurse asked from behind her mask, and you had the answer ready, but it got stuck on your lips and a coughing fit took over.

The fever stole away most of your time in hospital. You have faint memories of a razor-scaled snake sliding down the back of your throat; the feeling that your chest had been excavated and your lungs hung on the foot of your bed. You wanted to die, but they forced the air back into you.

how to gut a fish

They let you out when you could walk to the bathroom without stopping; your bed was needed for others. Afterwards, your throat hurt so badly from the tubes that you didn't speak for a week, but yellow posters screamed at you from every window.

You wonder if it was then, in the breathless dark of the viral ward, that your son's spine began to bend – the creeping twist that was only a shadow of suspicion as he began to crawl; your overactive imagination as he pulled himself upright; and the slow, grey hug of certainty that settled in after he complained about sitting up straight on his first day of school.

In the supermarket, you give Gideon his own list to check off, but he is too quick for you, finds everything while you are still dithering at the flour dispensers. He has requested a glittery ninja cake for his seventh birthday next week. You're out of practice but you'll give it a go; you hope it is enough to sate him, but know it will not be.

Roisín has taken up horse riding, and he wants lessons for his birthday. But you spent an hour in bed one night watching video compilations of riding accidents set to a laugh track. Again and again the riders fell – skulls met concrete, legs slipped under hooves, shoulders stretched from sockets – while the laughter bellowed and bounced. You sped the videos up and slowed them down again, dissecting each fall, mapping the twisting of bones. Finally, Art woke up with a snort, noticed the soft, flickering glow on your face and took your phone away.

An elderly woman keeps her distance at the top of the supermarket aisle until you've finished, impatiently scrolling through a stock-screen. Gideon comes around the corner too fast, but he deftly veers around her like they are opposing poles of a magnet.

You remember the girls in the playground and feel a quick and tight sadness that your son is so attuned to avoiding the closeness of others, that he lives in a safety bubble of his own creation, that he washes his hands before he hugs his grandfather.

———

You had seen your father upset before, at weddings or hurling matches, but never like this, his swollen eyes leaking tears like hot pus oozing from a wound.

Gideon had been in surgery for six hours already and your father had been calm and firm throughout, only messaging updates to his brother. In the waiting room, you dozed off against Art's shoulder, just for a second, because you hadn't slept the night before, the fortnight before, really, ever since you accompanied your son to the paediatric clinic to have a nurse take a half-pint of blood from his small body.

how to gut a fish

You had explained to him about this type of kindness; that he was donating the blood to himself, to help his body heal after his operation. He liked that idea and began to write notes to his future self, describing his new Pokémon runners; hoping that the legendary Pipaconch card would have come out by the time he was reading the letter.

You shouldn't have, you really shouldn't have, but you took the letters from his hiding place under the stairs and read them. You cried like a dog in the dimly lit hallway, while Art held your shoulders and made noises that sounded like static.

In the hospital, you opened your eyes and your father's face was a wine-blotched tablecloth against the white walls of the waiting room. Fear rippled out from him like a bear shaking off water and his closed-mouth sobs made awful, crooked shapes in the sanitised air.

You sighed then, quietly and gently, and began to melt into your seat. The breath came out of your lungs in a slow and steady stream, like you were sealing a sandwich bag for a picnic. You felt faintly sad that you were soon going to feel very sad, as if you were looking up into the shadow of a cresting wave, and then your jumper gathered against the cold plastic of the chair as you slid into darkness on the floor.

---

the skellington dance

Gideon can't decide what he wants for dinner, so you have a medley: dinosaur potato wedges, frozen broccoli, a round of cheese and soy sausages. He arranges his plate like a sous-chef and makes you add an artistic squiggle of ketchup. You pick a sprig of parsley from the windowsill and place it in the centre of the plate with a flourish.

Art comes in from work and doesn't kiss you on the cheek; you had bickered that morning, but you know that later he will roll over in his sleep and cradle you. The three of you watch a cartoon after dinner, and all the way up the stairs you argue about the mechanics of dragon-fire.

Art has a game he plays with Gideon before bed. You leave the room because you hate it, but you still watch from the hallway every time. He waits until Gideon has taken off his clothes, tossed them in the general direction of the laundry basket and laid out his pyjamas on his bed.

Now I just have to unzip your skin, he says. He purses his thumb and forefinger together and drags them down the pink length of Gideon's scar, from the nape of his neck to his tailbone, stopping at the waistband of his underpants.

Gideon pretends to step out of his skin like a boiler-suit and prances around as if he were left in only his bare bones.

The skellington dance, they call it.

how to gut a fish

Earlier, in the changing rooms, as you put on your togs, Gideon told you about a trick he had discovered. Shona was strapping armbands to Roisín's elbows, but your son had been a fish almost since the day he was born.

Mum, you can use the bubbles to breathe underwater.

You slide into the children's pool for a minute to watch him show you. The water is warm and shallow; it only comes up to the bend of your knees. A circle of jets pumps out gentle streams of air, and the surface fizzes like a hangover cure.

Gideon bellyflops under the water as Roisín begins to wail about the chafe of the armbands. He dives deeper, pressing his lips into a seal against the metal jet-valve, his little body pale against the navy tiles. You dig your fingers into your thighs to keep from reaching into the water, from tearing him out and up into your arms.

Your son has to flail to stay underwater, but he does it, manages to keep his wriggling body under for ten seconds, twenty, thirty – and something begins to happen to the knot of fear you swallowed when he was born: the knot that tightened when the GP first furrowed her eyebrows, when his hand went limp in yours as the anaesthetic took hold, when you ushered him into a place of steel and pain and tears.

the skellington dance

Gideon finally loses his grip on the valve; the bubbles push him away across the pool and he can't latch back on in time. His head breaks the blue surface of the water with his cloth hat slouched over his eyes. The victory smile on his face is an unravelling.

haptic

The moon is always one second old.

This fact frightens her, in a way she can't quite make fit; it feels sad and wide and too small of a sentence to have any real relevance to the four hard walls of reality around her. One second, it takes, for sunlight to bounce, flex and turn against the deep craters and lunar seas, wriggle its way down through black to navy to blue, and fall yellow to the surface of the Earth. The moon could have collapsed, turned green, exploded; it would take a second before it was known down here in the city, on this balcony among balconies, above the wallowing cousin-light of the streetlamps.

The tall apartment blocks are arranged in a semi-circle that shelters the balcony from all but the easterly winds that come in over the sea, and they are usually sluggish and vague if they manage to make it all the way in from the docklands. Although the air is still, the soft hiss of summer rain slips in and begins to percolate in the square courtyard. The white balcony tiles squeak under Sofia's laced-up boots, and her dark raft of hair starts to attract raindrops like static. She stubs out her borrowed cigarette against the wall, drops it in an attempt at a pot plant, swings the glass door back over and steps into the flat.

Things that have happened have already happened. That's another one, another sentence that grips in under her ribcage like two curved index fingers. Behind her, a thickening haze slides across the moon.

———

John's studio apartment has a low roof and the furniture is jumbled without walls to define rooms; the dining table crosses a tiled line into a wood-effect kitchen and a microwave is set on top of a wardrobe. A dark smudge of a double bed corners the far side of the flat, and a pair of tartan pyjamas have been roughly folded and stuffed under a baby-blue pillow. A faux leather couch sits at the centre of the room, bookended by two beanbags. Small ripples of conversation make a ring around a large, flat-panelled screen. John's four guests are kind; they have erected an invisible privacy wall and keep their attention contained to the living area, away from the finger-ironed bedsheets and grubby bedside locker.

They still haven't decided on a soundtrack for the birthday party. The mousepad is passed over and back while songs are displayed on the screen, belly-up, for inspection. *Naveed,* Andrea calls to the intern, stretching her arms above her head to crack her wrists, *just pick anything*; something fuzzy, something to chill to after a long week of work.

Naveed feels a pink heat in his belly with Andrea's attention on him, although she doesn't look up as she checks the time on her phone again. He takes the mouse from her lap, careful not to touch the fabric of her jeans. He becomes aware of the tight feel of his throat, thinks for a moment and then puts on a cool, coffee-shop jazz playlist in front of a looping video of a roaring fire. The others laugh and raise their hands to the digital flames, and he feels relief as their attention moves away from him.

———

Sofia slips off to the cubicle-sized bathroom to wash the faint orange tinge of the cigarette from between her two fingers. There is no window in John's bathroom, but it is brighter than the rest of the apartment, the tone changing from soft butter to a harsh fluorescence that beats at the dipped space above her right eyelid. When she lifts her hand to examine it in the mirror, the tarry V of her grandfather's digits is overlaid against her own image, and her tongue searches for the wood-sweet smoke of his fattened roll-ups. But she finds only staleness in her own mouth, so she takes a slug of mouthwash and a pump of lavender-scented soap, as slick and white as saliva.

John had done a quick clean before his guests arrived, swiping a cloth across the basin and the cistern; the track through the dust is clear, but curls of dark hair still spill out from a rusting electric razor on the single shelf. Sofía doesn't notice the leftover dust; she is performing an inspection: the mirror-face is sallow, washed-out, like a heavy coat that has spun in tumbling cycles for hours and has left a grey pool of water in the drum. Her foundation, applied on the commuter train that morning, has mixed with day-sweat and has dried into a firm, itching surface, and the prints of her fingers appear in the dark moons under her eyes.

She splashes water up her forearms and dabs it against the back of her neck. The taps on the basin are unfamiliar; the hot and cold flows are separated, but the steel is angled so they can come together into a single, lukewarm stream.

———

In the alcove of the kitchen, John fills his mother's shallow terracotta bowls with crisps made from lentils, curled shapes that dust his fingers red, then arranges a plate of chocolate marshmallows that are splitting at the seams. He cracks open a can of cider and lays out the snacks, then flops on a vintage blue-leather beanbag. He rises again straight away to flick on the heat; the draught from the balcony has caused the skin on Andrea's arms to goosepimple, but she isn't the type to complain, at least in person; a comment might be made on Monday about his cold apartment or a pointed sneeze unleashed at their lunch break.

The radiators begin to hum; Andrea sends him a smile but doesn't wait for it to be delivered. She is telling a story about an old friend who has taken up sea swimming, but the degrees of separation are too wide and John's attention frays.

Sofia has not yet come back from the bathroom. The beanbag shifts under John and he feels a sudden, dropped-belly fear; a fear that the voices that wait for him in the shower have broken loose and slipped out over the rim of the bathtub to trap her there. Lately the voices have been escaping from the shower and into other quiet places, into bus stops and queues and blank pauses in the middle of debugging sessions; he has taken to tapping a rhythm of twos and threes against his thigh to contain them, to stop them from breaking through and dragging him home.

Last time he had gone home, south and west into the flat belly of the Midlands, he had driven loops in his father's jeep, slowing as he passed his old neighbour-girlfriend's house. Her parents live alone there now; she is two kids deep in a council house in the next town over, and he sometimes laughs with others from his school about what he missed out on; he could've been set for life as a part-time publican, full-time dad; accompanied by an emoji with a slant for a mouth. But the warm heart of her still wakes him at night and he sees her black lick of eyeliner in calligraphy.

When he had broken into her at a house party, half a lifetime ago, he had been the more experienced, by a darkened fumble in a fairground car park, but the trust that came out of her in waves that night had followed him through every room of the party and caused him to throb and contract in turns. Frightened, he had drunk beer after beer and chased shots with strangers; plucked a half-smoked joint out from between a dosing metalhead's lips, but still her trust had come, had lapped up against him, easing him slowly but surely into somebody's spare room, on to somebody's hard sofa, into her soft gasp; a short, high noise that had almost made him burst on the spot. Recently he has realised that this moment was the pivot point, the swinging fulcrum of his life, and he has been tipping away from equilibrium ever since.

On his fourth pass in the jeep, it had grown dark, and when the light flicked on in her parents' upstairs landing, he had come awake and driven away and into the town. He had picked up a three-in-one at the local chipper and flown home down the back roads, taking

bends so fast they stopped being bends and straight-
ened themselves out into a flattened path of speed.
He had flicked the headlights on and off to see how
much his hands remembered, and they knew better
than his brain, which wanted to jerk at the wheel in
panic, but when he closed his eyes, his hands and feet
played the tune of a swallow high above the Atlantic,
and he made it home before the brown surface of the
curry even congealed.

In the kitchen, the conversation between his two
sisters and mother had circled around a dark pit of
washed porcelain saucers and scrubbed bedsheets,
their backs aching from bedsore lifts. The women
only leaned faintly on their words, but the compres-
sion was there – *why aren't you here, why don't you help,
why don't you stay* – and their voices now beat a tempo
against his skull every time he closes his eyes. He
had forced himself to eat in the sickroom and make
conversation, but he had to crack the sash window to
let in the night because his father's breath was an old,
dying tongue.

John shifts again on the beanbag. Sofia is still not
back from the bathroom. He sees the voices curling
under his Super Mario shower curtain and circling
her like wild, slat-ribbed dogs. He takes a long gulp
and the half-drunk can of cider buckles under the
pressure of his fingers. Callum taps the can in query;
six per cent alcohol but surprisingly sweet, John tells him.

how to gut a fish

Andrea sees the strain in John's jawbone and tells him to *keep on keeping on*, in a sing-song voice that raises the corners of his mouth, and as Sofia finally reappears from the bathroom she decides they have reached the unsteady tipping point of the evening and it is time to produce the birthday present from behind the couch. They had all chipped in for it, but it had been Andrea's idea; John is her second cousin, after all, although their mothers are separated by an ocean and an unresolved incident outside a rugby club disco.

The gift had been expensive, but she worries that their after-work gatherings are growing stale and listless; two of them are off the drink so there is a reluctance to spill too much, to find shadowed corners to sow secrets, to trust in what is said or heard. Andrea knows her face softens and becomes magnetic in the dark space after midnight, like the untouched surface of margarine. On nights out, she sits in booths with friends and gathers their heartaches like collectibles. She rises early the next day to do hill sprints and sweat out the alcohol; she senses the bolt-upright waking of others at around eleven in the morning and basks in the heat of their shame.

The group message with the suggested contribution had sounded like a dread foghorn in her friends' pockets as they considered the price of declining, except for Naveed, who was just happy to be included. But Andrea is too discreet for secret-spilling; she keeps the thousand slices of other people's sadness she has collected to herself, only rifling through them as dawn creeps in and her boyfriend snorts in his sleep.

Callum had been the last to reply, with three thumbs-up, preceded by a shocked face at the price. But nobody really minds because the entire company is doing well, and the money comes and goes each month like a rising tide; Andrea sometimes buys desserts at the canteen and leaves them untouched on the red, star-shaped tables meant to encourage conversation. Her boyfriend tells her she is terrible at budgeting; that their forever-home with a front garden and backyard shed will stay on the pages of her forever-notebook, but to her, money is just numbers on a screen; black lines that wiggle and cringe.

She keeps an assortment of old Irish punts in the bottom of her jewellery box, waiting for them to appreciate. Sometimes she sketches the designs of the coins in her notebook: salmon, bull, horse, bird and stag.

The present isn't wrapped, but John keeps his eyes closed as he fingers the box and makes a guess or two before opening them to feign confusion, even though Andrea knows he recognises the slick black branding. He mock-gasps – *this is too much, much too much, I'm too old for toys!* – but still a gentle warmth of gratitude settles over the room, and he smiles at each of his friends in turn, even Naveed, who he has only met twice before. Andrea makes a cutting shape in the air with her left hand and goes to pour herself a gin and tonic; her part is done, and she adds the wet blinking of John's eyes to her collection.

———————

The virtual reality set is a matte coal colour, slotted into a white nest of polystyrene fenders. Two handpieces sit alongside a bulky visor attached to a headset, and Callum pulls them out with a careful reverence, then pretends to fumble each piece in turn. Naveed had once used his friend's VR kit back in Toronto, so he is nominated to set it up. He is glad to find a use for his hands which have suddenly grown heavy; untethered and alien. He arranges cables and installs the program as the others discuss the applications of augmented reality.

Callum tells of a therapist he once visited, who had suggested an immersive exposure to bees; an attempt to shift a decades-old fear implanted by a scene in *My Girl* (a young Macaulay Culkin's best role, in his humble opinion). They argue about virtual sex; deciding that 360-degree porn is try-it-once material, but attachments or plug-in accessories are a leap too far into the bizarre; and *so* unhygienic, Andrea adds.

Naveed thinks of his first girlfriend as he waits for the progress bar to fill. She had lived in the dorm below him for the last year of university and had been born with a slight cleft in the right side of her mouth that had given her a permanent, unprovoked sneer. They had met at a Marvel midnight screening, and in the flickering light of the basement cinema he had thought about easing the head of his penis into the curved space between her teeth and upper lip, but gently, pink kissing pink. The thought had squirmed at the back of his scalp as they sat in a diner and she ate sweet potato chips off his plate one at a time; had kept him awake on the coffee-coloured couch the night she had let him stay over, but after he left the next morning before breakfast she had stopped replying to the funny videos he sent her.

By the time the internship came up in Dublin he had decided that she had probably never been his girl-friend at all, and he had forgotten about her until this moment; an eruption, the vast possibilities of digital sex toys. He sees her purple-brown mouth enclosed in plastic, a fish-hook arch in her upper lip, extending from a darkened cable.

The virtual reality program finishes downloading and the large screen finally fumbles to life; a stuttering clap from the others for a scarlet Naveed. They stand to get fresh drinks and rearrange cables, then sit again in a small circle, making barricades out of footstools. John stands in the cleared centre and forces little gunshot laughs down through his nose as he drops the visor over his eyes. The two black handles fit gently into the curve of his palms, and he falls into a darkness deafened by the noise-cancelling headset. Inside the headpiece, a *welcome* message pops up. Naveed adjusts some settings as the others point at the TV screen, which is displaying the stream from the inside of the visor; *John-o-vision*, jokes Callum.

Suddenly, the surface of an alien planet appears, and John stumbles in the dry, virtual air. His stomach wrinkles as he turns his head in a silent circle; the others follow the path of his eyes on the screen. All around him, reddened cliffs crack against the horizon; soil like fork-patterned pastry chases endless spouts of rock and vast, dry oceans. In the sky, a low moon zips by, and another moon, further out, performs a slower, solemn orbit.

He takes a cautious step, points a controller and leaps forward a hundred belly-swooping metres across the surface of Mars, stumbling into hour-glass-shaped sand ridges and volcanoes larger than a country. A metallic Rover appears to keep pace beside him like a dog, wittering in beeps and dashes, a song of eager concern. From the couch, the others point at the screen and direct him forward, back-ward – *watch out for the table*, Callum pleads – but John doesn't hear him. He hears no voices at all, only the lonely whistling of Martian winds. His heart rate steadies and slows as he lets out a heavy breath.

But a prickling strangeness begins to grow; the sense of being alone in a stranger's house. The sun that stretches over the aching deserts is low and small, a smallness that is wrong, and it shunts his heart off to one side. The handles tremble against the firm grip of his knuckles as a dust storm begins to whip the reddened air.

John pulls the goggles away from his eyes, blinking in the unfamiliar light of his own apartment. He raises the headset to the others in query. Callum is nearest, but he holds out his palms in a way that displays the tendons in his wrists and pleads motion sickness.

He launches into a story about an incident of projectile vomit on a Florida rollercoaster; a walking cliché of a Yank who had caught it between the slop of her breasts and called him a pussy for sicking up. He had been too shaken from the loops and spins to apologise, and she had followed him on tree-trunk thighs to the restrooms; calling *faggot, faggot, faggot* all the way, until a costumed pirate had taken her by the elbow and spun her into a parade. Andrea groans with laughter and Naveed rolls his eyes with the exasperation of continental proximity.

how to gut a fish

Callum sits back and lets the story be passed around, the others offering up their own theme-park experiences. He feels safer, now, as if he has had some toxic part of him removed. He is one of them, even though he is almost a decade older than these twenty-somethings, and he feels it in the sweat-damp pate of his balding skull – has it gotten warmer or is it the beer? But he still tastes the ebb of an uneasy tide and he swallows the sight of the horrible mass of cables like a strangely shaped piece of meat. The screen is still lit up; brave new planets are waiting to be explored, but the thought of turning in a blind, vulnerable circle under the eyes of the others is a shivering, dizzying prospect, like the grunt of an unwelcome lover over dipped and sweating shoulders.

He hardly knows the others, really, although he sits with John and Sofía sometimes at lunch on their company's sprawling campus, and he had tearfully told Andrea about his ex-boyfriend's eyes at the last work barbecue, borrowing her lip liner to demonstrate the squashed-olive shape on a napkin. But needs must: the friends he had entered the company with five years ago have moved on, tired of dizzying numbers and designated fun. They bumped into other people and didn't bump away again; moved to a commuter belt, or to a small village in north-west France, or to Taiwan – the to was never as important as the from. Now, he prefers to sit to one side of the conversation, attached but adjacent, because these ones will leave him too, for lower salaries and fewer perks but for an office that has four solid walls and less space for brainstorming, no on-site masseuse or dental benefits. Instead they will find co-workers to comfortably hate, a photocopier that half-works; a light and a job that switches off at the end of the day.

When the conversation trails away, John gestures again with the headset. *No*, Callum says, *definitely not for me*, and points instead at Sofia, whose face has slouched into a hammock of thought. Her eyes flick on and she stands up; a swallowing back of spit, of tightness, of undoing.

Way, the others say, *w-a-aay*, stretching out the word as curse or encouragement; the hooting of mutinied sailors, relieved from attention.

Naveed dismisses the red surface of Mars, opens another program and loads up a darkened Earth, spins the globe on its axis to pass a day, a year; reverses time and flips the poles. The colour spills out of his eyes like a brown tea blot and he leans back on his hips; *if you want*, he tells her, *only if you want*.

Sofia carefully takes the headset in both hands and stares into the cup of the visor, the leftover warmth of John's skin rising from the padding. Naveed signs her in, sets up a new profile, fills up blank boxes with her details. *Where to?* he asks, as she settles the head-piece over her eyes. The memory of a cigarette drifts in from the balcony door, kept ajar by a heavy, antique kitchen iron.

Home.

The word comes out as a question, testing the air, tugging on the thread that flies across the vast, vast ocean, skates down the crenellations of the mountains and out across a flat, green sea. It pulls along a concrete corridor of traffic dressed with scales of corrugated iron, into a cement-poured town of square streets and dust; the river-split neighbourhoods lit up in yellow and pink; a library that only opens on Saturdays and *arepa* stalls that never close; blue-gilled iguanas cling-ing to *chontaduro* trees; the taste of crude oil when the hot wind blows in from the plains; a sun that rises and sets at the same time each day as easily and smoothly as the night-breath of a child.

Home is where the visor brings her, to the road outside her family's farm, low-roofed and squatting under the blazing sun. Their dog is there, frozen on the screen, in a blur that stretches his tail out into a comet, turned slightly to watch the camera-car passing. The dog has been in the cold ground for three years – lymphoma and a heart that couldn't stay awake – but he is still here now, in this everlasting now, snapshotted against the white brick walls of the *finca*.

haptic

There is the patch of fruit trees that never dropped pure oranges, rather mottled greens and blacks and blues; they split on her grandfather's *machete* in bloody eruptions; her little sister shrieking *otra vez!* He could sit as still as a summer cloud until the last second, then spin his short, yellow fingers up and around so the blade leaped like a river fish over a rock, silver-scaled and panicked to find itself in the air. The fruit would be sliced into two perfect halves of flesh and pulp, but sometimes if it had sat too long in the sun it would hit the blade side-on and there would be an explosion of wasps; black and yellow vipers that whirred away in fury.

Only seconds have passed. The headset has just settled into place; John is still stepping away, hands dropping to his side. Sharp, glass-edged water pricks at Sofia's eyes and the high pant of noise that comes out of her is a decision undone, the reversal of time, the dead come to life; a hearty, gasping, disbelieving cry.

Home, *corazón*. The word is a heart.

red market

PLEASE — NO SOILED GOODS.
ITEMS IN GOOD WORKING ORDER ONLY.
CLOTHING SHOULD BE WASHED
AND IRONED.
CONTACT AGATHA FOR MORE DETAILS.

The men come with their vans early on Saturday morning and dislodge piles of furniture like undigested chunks of bone. The pavement outside the building gradually fills up, becoming a child's playground of tables and chair sets. The workers manoeuvre a set of bedframes — not quite a pair, but laid out top to tail they almost fit each other; a few wooden slats are missing from one but they can be easily replaced, a €20 discount at most. The men unload a purple futon with beaded embellishments on the arms depicting the Virgin Mary with pink cheeks and a baby-blue shawl. The sky above is crisp and clear so far and the market will be busy this weekend; Christmas is only a week away.

how to gut a fish

The large, high-ceilinged warehouse echoes as boxes are brought in and unpacked, but as the room begins to fill up with people the noise becomes more contained. Thirteen off-brand messenger bags are carried in on a sack barrow and laid out on a waiting table. A woman untangles a pile of semi-silk scarves and hangs them from the rafters above her stall. She fills two metal racks with wedding dresses in shades ranging from grey smoke and eggshell to ivory and alabaster. A prized evening suit, made entirely out of snakeskin, is hung on a hanger above a doorframe; a man sets out a sign that reads NO TIME WASTERS. Beneath it, carved out of dark wood, a chest-high statue of Freddy Mercury preens, mouth open in eternal song.

A shallow podium sits at the centre of the hall with a red tin box chained to the floor beside it. On a folding table, bidding papers are stacked beside a DISPLAY ONLY sign. A stout, serious woman, Marci by her nametag, places a striped throw across the podium, and arranges a set of Le Creuset roasting trays that had come in after the closure of an old café on Clanbrassil Terrace. Beside them, on a chest-high railing, she places a particularly nice pair of designer trousers that mimic the falling fabric waves of a skirt. She straightens a selection of gold necklaces on a display rack and secures the chains at the back with a cable tie.

red market

Marci steps back to survey the scene and stretches her index fingers and thumbs, bringing them together to make a frame. She checks her watch and calls to her twin daughters, who are restless and bickering already; their classes finished for the Christmas holidays on Friday and she dreads the thought of two whole weeks off school. Finally, after conferring with a few others, Marci directs a pair of young men to wheel in an antique diving suit, complete with weighted boots. The suit is arranged on one side of the podium; the centre is left bare. The helmet is tarnished, but the copper gleam is visible underneath, and the air around it tastes like blood.

The sun crests the roof and the final shutters go up as Aindriú, the building manager, arrives with his teenage nephew. He shows the acne-scarred boy around the market, then sends him up to the office overlooking the open plain of the warehouse to set up his computers. The boy trips on the first of the perforated metal steps, but his uncle is kind enough to pretend not to notice. Below the office, white sheets are whipped off stalls. Strong coffee is brewed in a large, scaled pot, and the hard scent of it takes the edge off the morning.

Half an hour later, a blue Berlingo takes the turn off the main road slowly, letting a pair of walkers pass in front of it, even though the pedestrian light is blinking red. The van backs up to the side of the building; parking is not yet a problem, but by noon the street outside the market will be wedged with cars and bicycles and electric scooters. George gets out of the Berlingo and stretches his legs before walking over to a group of yawning stallholders; for the occasion, he has agreed to put on a red suit and false beard and sit outside on a marble bench. He pokes a friend in his over-hanging gut, *after my job, eh,* but the movement is familiar and expected, so the man dodges the full force of the jab. They laugh for a few minutes together and briefly swap stories before turning to unload the contents of the van.

The young girl's elbows are bound together behind her back. Her shoulder blades are sharpened like the wings of a moth, and her ankles are tied to her wrists. The men carry her to the podium under Marci's direction, and the girl is placed belly-down in the centre, in between the diving helmet and the roasting trays. The bungee cords wrapping her body are admired – *you never know you need them until you really need them, isn't that always the way?* – and a few people stop to pluck the green-striped elastic out from the ridges of her skin to test the bounce. The flesh beneath them is white but blood rushes in as soon as the pressure is lifted; they snap back into a slightly different position and begin new ridges. Her thighs are held in place with heavy ratchet straps, bookended with metal clasps that are rusting around the edges. The orange bands are the strongest, the label advises, grey for medium-sized burdens, and blue for restraining small objects, 10 kilos max. The girl expands her ribcage as far as it will go to test the chafe of the binding.

George stretches again and prepares to go upstairs to change into his outfit. He pauses on the steel steps up to the office, considers for a moment, and returns to the girl on the podium. His eyesight isn't getting any better – *if you're not in, you can't win, isn't that it?* – so he fills out a slip of paper with his name, address and bid and places it into the red box. The girl raises her head into a stiff smile for him as he walks away. She opens her mouth but only a dry, croaking sound comes out: her vocal cords have been numbed with an anaesthetic spray. Customs and Excise are difficult at the best of times, and George has made this journey enough times to smooth out any lumps and bumps in advance.

———

More people begin to trickle in as the market officially opens and the crisp Saturday lengthens towards lunchtime; five, ten, twenty, and suddenly there is no more time for talking, only business. The crowds roil and flow around the stalls.

A woman, fat and greying, roams the vintage clothing aisles, searching for conversation; *isn't this lovely, who would give this away, are you here every week?* Her feet are too swollen for anything but house slippers and her cardigan sleeves bulge with tissues; clean and folded in the right sleeve, used and crumpled in the left. She is deaf in one ear and announces this at every opportunity, turning her head to one side like a sparrow when she speaks. She stops to lift the lid off the largest roasting tray on the podium and look into its red-stained belly. The girl shifts amiably on her stomach to make room, but the woman has no interest in flesh today, only company. Besides, the girl's dark skin is paler than usual from the weeks it has been occluded in the journey, but still not light enough for the red market.

Outside, imitation snow is pumped from a machine into an area that has been cordoned off for children to flutter and pose beside life-sized cut-outs of frozen cartoon princesses. In his Father Christmas costume, George is doling out fistfuls of chocolate coins; *knee-sitting's out of the question these days, it's all gone politically correct*, he winks to a watching parent who is straining to look casual. Christmas songs hang in the air and the outdoor stalls sparkle with an assortment of angels, wooden snowflakes that smell like cedar and plastic candy canes that can be personalised with a loved one's name.

For lunch, there is winter vegetable soup from a tureen, €6 per cup, and sourdough bread rolls €4 extra. A mobile falafel van pulls up between a solid-shampoo retailer and a CBD oil and cosmetics stall. On a windowsill, a platter of yesterday's vegan pastries begins to sag in the centre; a man feeds a home-made raisin flapjack to his dog. There is watered-down mulled wine and a brazier for roasting chestnuts; the white flesh crumbles between the fingers of children, chalky and sweet.

The afternoon brings a heavy shower of rain that straddles the market for almost two hours. An awning is rolled out, but the majority of commerce moves inside. Condensation drips against the windows and the smell of wet wool becomes unbearable. The few new shoppers that appear do so only for shelter, and make repeated loops around the indoor stalls to kill time before the rain ends. Some stop to admire the girl on the podium. A student nurse fingers a foot-long scar that crests across the girl's exposed abdomen. *Pity*, she thinks, *the left is usually the stronger.* Marci opens her palms in a helpless motion when questioned about the missing kidney; it is difficult to get undamaged goods these days, but the stitches are neat and old; besides, the girl is in good health. The student nurse considers degrees of weaknesses as she does one more loop around the market, but she returns to put in a bid for the other kidney; her uncle has been in dialysis for years and is running out of time.

how to gut a fish

Evening crawls in, but closing time is jagged and uneven, depending on how cold each vendor's feet are and what is waiting for them at home for dinner. Sheets are stretched over piles of kitchen utensils and bootleg DVDs; bumbags are emptied and sales totted up. The outdoor stalls are stripped bare, warned by the earlier downpour and the wet melt of cardboard on the pavement. Inside, the last browser, oblivious to the falling stutter of background hum, finishes a lazy lap around the few remaining undraped stalls.

Marci calls to her daughters to come in from the cold, and goes up the stairs to collect her things from the office. While they wait, the twins paint each other's nails with rainbow glitter polish; they are on the index finger of the bound girl's second hand by the time their mother returns and shoos them away. Marci taps a syringe and inserts it into the girl's left flank, massaging the skin in concentric circles, and her eyelids begin to droop. The twins play a twisting, flailing game with colourful scarves, draping them around their heads. Marci switches off the radio as the three of them leave the warehouse, and the web of fairy lights goes dark.

Aindriú comes by to pick up his nephew and lock up for the day, calling a low *halloooo* across the darkened hall to make sure there is nobody left in the shadows. The boy averts his eyes from the girl on the podium, blushing as he clatters down the stairs and crosses the room to meet his uncle. Aindriú turns the keys of the front and back doors, rattling them to be sure, then loops a thick padlock around the main gates. He drops his nephew home, but first they stop at the chipper for a battered sausage and a shared portion of chunky chips.

At dusk, starlings begin to flit to an ancient assortment of nests that sit just under the eaves; the dark smudges of mud and straw are renewed by the birds every year. Inside the silent building, the space heaters flick on, storing up warmth for the morning. The girl's skin begins to goosepimple under her own white sheet. Rust-coloured urine trickles down the inside of her right thigh and seeps to the edge of the podium; it will have dried completely by morning.

At midnight the building shifts as a teenager slams his fist against the corrugated iron at the back. His not-quite-girlfriend laughs; the weed has made her lightheaded although she can usually hold herself together better than he can. The boy rattles at the door-chain in a half-hearted way and sits down on an old pink tricycle that has remained unsellable through the long, wet summer and autumn. The girl becomes hysterical at the sight of his knees folded up to his shoulders, and she staggers against the side of the building, gasping with laughter. He manages to reach the pedals and cycles, squeaking, for a minute or two, saluting her as she slides down to her bottom, taking shrieking in-breaths and covering her eyes. He gets off the bike, managing to sit on his own testicles in the process, and she laughs harder, before dropping her cold fingers into his trousers to massage the injured pieces of him. He quivers with pain but lets her continue; his mother has stayed at home every night this week and hates the sight of his girlfriend for no reason he can decipher. Inside the building, the girl's painted fingernails catch the rising of the moon and glitter like a galaxy reflected in a dark pool of water.

Around five in the morning, a fox slinks its way through the narrow railings and makes a leisurely circuit of the outdoor area. It stops to dig a shallow hole in a pile of imitation snow, a shock of blue-white powder under the low, orange clouds. The fox's fur is oil-slick from the earlier rain and it screams frustration at the faint scent of a younger male that had passed by a few days before. This banshee call causes the girl to shift beneath the surface of wakefulness, but some faint kindness keeps her under.

Just before dawn, a streak-chested owl plunders the starling nests, flitting from hatchling to hatchling, pulling out grey tufts of feathers and plucking red fibre from their breastbones. The market's new CCTV system catches the display on night-vision camera and the footage will go briefly viral online a month later as an example of nature's brutality; Aindriú's nephew will be able to enhance the video to the point that the quick darting of the owl's beak becomes clear, a yellow needlepoint on the end of a darkened hook.

An hour after dawn on Sunday, the first van pulls up outside the gates again with more items for sale. It unloads a set of paired futons, two black bags of clothes for sorting and a stack of 1950s pornography magazines. Aindriú is late – his cat had woken him early and he had fallen back into a heavy sleep – but he appears with the keys in the time it takes the delivery men to smoke two cigarettes. More vans appear and restocking begins in earnest. The carved wooden birdhouses have been particularly popular, labelled AUTHENTIC BAVARIAN OAK but really made of plywood cast-offs from a workshop down the road. Jars of cosmetics with added fresh Irish peat are stacked in a high pyramid like soup cans, and a fill-your-own teabag station is restocked from large sacks of loose leaves.

By the time the lights come on in the building, the girl's breath is a slow wheeze; the stretching of her arms behind her back has spread out her lungs into flattened slabs, and each inflation is an effort. White foam corners her mouth as white sheets whip off the stalls, and she has defecated on herself. Marci yawns as she walks the aisles between stalls, aiming a bottle of air freshener above her head and letting out spurts every couple of seconds. She notices the foul smell as she passes the podium and thinks for a moment – *sure there's only the rest of the day to get through* – and an extra layer of lavender-scented mist falls on the strapped-down figure.

The crowds are slower this morning; the initial panicked rush of the weekend has eased. The first sale of the day is a man's designer jacket, extra wide at the shoulders. The left-hand side of the jacket is flecked with white hairs from the previous owner's terrier. There are a pair of reading glasses in the front pocket and a handful of glucose sweets, but the buyer will not notice until he tries it on for a friend's commitment ceremony in February.

There is an outflow of people for Sunday Mass at the local church before eleven; a skeleton crew is left to mind the stock. Bartering is suspended under strict instructions; prices are firm in the hands of these caretakers. Taking advantage of the lull, small sheaves of money are folded and coins changed for notes. The red box continues to fill with shy bids. In the distance, the church bell sings out, echoed by the tolling of the Angelus on the battered radio.

A part-time wigmaker arrives around lunchtime. He had seen the market advertised on a friend's social media feed, but the girl's hair is shorter than it appeared in the picture and too curly besides. It would brighten and smooth with some shea butter, but the lack of care shown in the shipping of the product is annoying enough for him to leave, disappointed, without placing a bid. He pauses to look at a bird's nest of cables and dislodges a PlayStation 4 controller and a disembowelled Xbox. His eldest son is showing an interest in computers, and a project could be just the thing to make him forget about the beer. His fingers trace wires, matching female to male, HDMI to VGA. He presses his lips against an old Nintendo 64 game to blow out the dust and the wet warmth of his spittle settles on the copper bars of connection.

Buried in a box of tchotchkes, a set of three black minstrels in miniature with white eyes and swollen red slugs for lips. The musicians stand together in bright blue suits on a heavy plaster base, leaning out from a central point like the fronds of a plant. One bares white teeth at an old-fashioned microphone, another's cheeks bulge around a trombone, while the third grips a double bass between his knees. A dark-skinned child fingers their jet-black, rounded hair; his mother slaps his hand away and drags him into the next room to measure his feet against a pair of slate-grey patent school shoes. The boy stops to stare instead at the Tupperware containers filled with penny sweets – liquorice, cola bottles, red jellies and gobstoppers.

At the podium, nobody has been brave enough to try the antique diving helmet on, despite Marci's showman-like urgings. An installation artist, having seen it advertised on the market's website, comes by just to inspect it, stepping around the girl's bound ankles to get a better look. He pulls open the hinge with two fingers; the glass of the viewing pane is clouded with trapped underwater breath. But the artist had a panic attack earlier in the week and the thought of actually bidding makes his throat tighten, so he doesn't ask about the price and leaves instead, furious with himself. A week later, he will wake gasping in the night, having dreamed his skull has been forced up into the helmet, collapsed and become malleable, like that of a cuttlefish.

———

At the end of the day, the pile of porn magazines is picked up by a long-haired youth in a corduroy jacket; he likes the idea of papering the walls of his band's practice space with breasts and penises and dark tufts of body hair. The band members will rotate in and out due to a fractious lead singer, and each will add adornments to the walls: sharpie moustaches, boot marks, and palm-blood from a snapped guitar string.

Come closing time at six o'clock, the outer gates to the warehouse are locked behind the last browsers. The girl's chest has almost stilled. Marci bends to rest the back of her hand against her cheek and raises a small make-up mirror in front of the girl's mouth to check her breath. Moving briskly, she opens the red tin box chained to the podium, and her two young daughters help to count out the slips of paper into piles, while Aindriú's nephew tallies the online interest from the upper office. This is the first year the market has accepted web bids; a few stakeholders were uncertain, but the offers have increased exponentially and the security questions seem to have filtered out most of the time-wasters.

The fresh corpse settles and sighs as Marci removes the glittering nail varnish with white spirit, exasperated by her daughters' interference, but feeling a gentle warmth for them all the same. Outside, George sweeps the boot-scuffed mess of fake snow back into a pile and has just finished hoovering it up when Aindriú returns from dropping his nephew home. Together, they go inside, hoist the girl's body on to their shoulders, careful to avoid the stains on her thighs. They carry her up the stairs and into the office for the final tally.

The organs – kidneys, liver, lungs and heart – have performed well, as expected, *snapped up like an air fryer in Aldi!* Marci jokes to Aindriú.

George has missed out on winning the corneas, but there has been a stroke of luck – the two highest bidders have bid the same amount, and if Marci contacts them each will likely overbid again, sensing the closeness of seeing.

how to gut a fish

The girl was young, so her eggs are in demand, but the winning bid is from a fertility clinic that buys up the entire stock, although an undiagnosed case of polycystic ovary syndrome means that the eggs will underperform; three couples will weep in the night after the news is broken.

There is low demand for blood at the moment, as supplies are healthy, so the girl's will be drained and set aside in plastic blood-bags, just in case. In two months, a pile-up on the M50 will upset the delicate rhizome of the donation system, but it will be too late; forty-two days is the maximum shelf-life for human blood.

The lights in the building stay on late into Sunday night, pressing against the office windows, black shadows passing behind the frosted glass like inverted exclamation marks. Finally, the strange alchemy of flesh to coin is completed and the packages are wrapped and set aside. The numbers are totted up and divided, and divided again. A small sum of money is earmarked to be transferred back along the weaving path of the Berlingo, the shipping container, across the Continent and back into a tiny village where two brothers can now afford to go to school, and a mother will weep for her daughter every night for ten years until her heart clogs and falls to pieces while she is crossing a busy road.

In the morning, what is left of the carcass will be put in a net and anchored in the river – a small tributary of the Liffey, but hip-height in places – where bacteria and fish will whittle it down to a loose pile of flesh and bones. Afterwards, the pulp will be boiled in caustic soda to dissolve any remaining meat, before the marrow is extracted for later use. Sunlight is best for removing the yellowish tint from the bones, but the weather has turned foul again, so a pair of UV lamps will be used instead, and the windows of the upstairs office will be taped over with bin bags. The bones will cure and whiten in a week, and a quick polish with the finest sandpaper will make them shine.

The skeleton will be sold to a medical school where it will be reassembled and strung on to a nylon wire frame. It will sit in the back of a classroom; students will draw eyelashes on it and pose it with its hands on its hips. Eventually, the metal wires in place of tendons and ligaments will rust and the bones will come loose. The skeleton will be sent to a new market, in pieces, and after a scrub to clean away the scales and dust of the classroom, it will be threaded back together along new wires, fibreglass this time.

It will hang straight and true in the centre of the red market, and it will shine.

Harlow

His mother had a choice between keeping the monkey or having the baby. She told the story often, in company, with a roll of her eyes and a helpless grin, as if this was the sore spot, the branching crossroads where her life had gone wrong.

The story morphed a little over the years, but kept the same approximate shape, like the course of a flood-prone river. She had been twenty-nine, volunteering in a wildlife sanctuary and staying in a Quechua community on the border of the Amazon. Her job, among a handful of other dislocated young Americans, had been to feed, bathe and socialise the orphaned primates.

One particular monkey had latched on to her so tightly that it followed her all around the complex, hanging from her shoulders like a furry backpack. They had been inseparable; devising a system of hand signals to communicate, sleeping together in her narrow hammock. Once, the young monkey woke screeching in the night, and she flicked on a light to find a Brazilian wandering spider perched on her hiking boots, its front legs raised in a defensive arch.

At first, his mother hadn't realised she was pregnant, and had worked at the sanctuary for a few more months until the problem became impossible to ignore. Then came a bouncing trip in the back of a jeep to the embassy in Quito – more of a closet than an embassy at that point, really – and a hastily arranged ticket for a flight home to a pair of disapproving parents in Indiana. But she had changed her mind in the airport and had instead hopped on a chartered Cessna to detour to Atlanta – you could do that type of thing in the seventies, she claimed – so her son Marc had been born in a Fulton County hospital, in the great state of Georgia, USA. Or was it DeKalb? She couldn't be sure.

When he was small, Marc asked her why she hadn't brought the monkey back with her. They could have dressed it up in his old clothes and sent it to school as his brother. They had moved about so much that whenever they stopped for a couple of years, Marc was always the weird kid with the American accent, so it wouldn't have made much difference to his social standing. He and the monkey could have held hands at zebra crossings and dominated the trapeze bars at the playground. Marc would draw wistful pictures of them together; himself with long, awkward limbs and corkscrew curls, the monkey with a white bandit mask around its eyes and a striped tail that stretched around the little crayon boy's shoulders.

In his mother's retellings, the exact species of the orphaned monkey changed too, from capuchin to squirrel to macaque. At a particularly wine-soaked dinner party when Marc was fifteen, he had challenged her on the contradictions. She had waved her arms at him in tight circles, as if she was washing two portholes on a cruise ship, and insisted it didn't matter; it was all the same monkey. Anyway, she went on, what she remembered most was its heart-wrenching howl as she left the compound for the last time. And, to the laughter of the red and shiny guests, the story's punchline was brought out again: it was the monkey or the baby; the rolling eyes and the smile.

He tells the story to Francine in his London apartment one night, as she slides her underwear back over her legs.

'And she would say this in front of you?' She huffs downwards through her nose. 'That's a bit cruel.'

He tries to explain that his mother didn't have an intentionally cruel bone in her body – rather, it was a problem of depth perception, a misunderstanding of scale – but Francine isn't listening. She has pulled out her phone and is reading about animal sanctuaries in Ecuador, and soon disappears into a deep-dive article on the links between private zoos and the drug trade in the Americas.

'Did you know that Pablo Escobar had four pet hippos that went wild after he was killed?' The light

of the phone on her face makes her look furious. 'Now there're hundreds of them. People think they're lucky.'

As soon as Marc heard the American accent on the phone, he felt a sense of resignation settle over him like a freshly cracked egg. The police officer was very sorry to inform him that his mother had had a massive stroke in a Walmart in western Virginia. The attending doctor said that her death was instantaneous and painless, if that gave him any solace.

It didn't. Marc looked around his London apartment, and everything seemed unfamiliar and strange. On the top of the stove, a silvery coffee pot was grumbling its way to the boil. The slightly curved screen of his laptop blinked at him in disbelief. Outside, on the street, two people were shouting at each other in a flat and bored way, as if from a great distance.

His mother was dead. He knew she would be furious that she hadn't gone out in a blaze of glory, giving her life to some great cause, like blocking the construction of an oil pipeline or reporting on an anti-imperialist guerrilla war.

But that had always been the problem. She had a heart as big and billowing as a rainbow spinnaker, but she couldn't fold it up enough to care about the little causes. The cause of buying new runners instead of stapling the old ones back together again. The cause of using the detergent that didn't trigger embarrassing rashes. The cause of remembering your son's girl-friends' names. The cause of making soft noises at all the right times.

On the phone, the officer continued to speak about arrangements and procedures, the practical trappings of death. But all Marc could see was his mother in a supermarket aisle, deliberating over ready meals, eyes darting from label to label, frozen for eternity in indecision.

He cut the officer off to ask what had been in her shopping basket when she died. The cop said he would check, in a kind voice he probably saved up for grief-mad strangers.

In the loft of her digs, Nina tells him about a scientist called Harry Harlow who had done experiments on monkeys and mothers, while she circles her fingers through his chest hair. Did he feel he always had to act up, to entertain his mother, to make up for the loss of her freedom?

Nina is in her second year of a sociology PhD and the crudeness of the analysis annoys him. 'Obviously it's a complex,' he tells her angrily, 'and a stupidly lazy one. It's like dreaming that you're falling before you get on a long plane journey. Your subconscious should have to put in a bit of effort.'

She pulls a handful of his hair tight around her fingers, but he barely notices the sting. 'Abuse or alcoholism or psychosis — I could deal with those. But how do you

*therapise this out of yourself? The shrink doesn't need
to do any damn work — the monkey represents a literal
fucking monkey.'*

He flew over to collect his mother's ashes from
Virginia on an airline that went into liquidation soon
afterwards. He heard the news on the radio while
waiting in the coroner's office for the few belongings
she had on her when she died. He wasn't surprised;
there had been a tension coming from the airline
staff, the feeling of a half-hour before closing time
on a rowdy week-night, when drinks were still being
poured but the countdown to last orders had begun.

The small, tall house she had rented outside
Roanoke only had three rooms, two below and one
above, and everything downstairs seemed to have
gravitated towards that natural state of being, the
heap. The landlord had a lot to say on the topic of
his mother, seeming to think that they were two co-
conspirators in cataloguing her life. But Marc felt
oddly protective of her things, at least until they
reached their final resting place. He shut the door on
the grinning man's face and got to work, filling his
rental car with black plastic bags in order to make the
ten-mile round trip to the municipal dump.

He was as ruthless and unsentimental with her
belongings as he knew she would have been. A hair-
dresser had once presented her with an envelope of

dark curls from his very first salon haircut at the age of six. She had put them in the compost heap when they got home and asked him to consider leaving his hair to grow long, so he could donate it to cancer survivors.

In a hotel bed in Soho, Artur just laughs and tells him he'll look good with a tail; that he knows an exclusive club they could go to if he wants to try it out. He uses his index fingers to draw large circles around Marc's eyes and pulls his top and bottom eyelids apart to make them bulge. 'I can see you as a sexy lemur,' he grins.

When Marc settled in London at the age of twenty-two to take up a horribly boring business degree, his mother had moved back to the States, as if to make a point. She had initially gone over to explore a Cherokee family connection, that much he knew, although he doubted her welcome had been one-sixteenth as gushing as she had expected. He felt he almost knew what she was trying to prove by moving away from him, but he didn't want to poke too hard at her reasoning, in case it resolved into a shape he was expected to do something with.

Marc had gotten on with his life, wandering on a gentle incline from one dull, well-paid job to another, trying to dilute any hereditary flightiness with spreadsheets and data files. He bought an apartment on the edge of Soho for a ridiculous amount of money, stripped it back to sharp lines and exposed wood, and then went about spending as little time as possible in it. A decade passed, punctuated by trips each way across the Atlantic once or twice a year. He and his mother usually only lasted a few days in each other's company, before wild, accusatory cries went up from both parties and flights were inevitably rebooked and brought forward.

But then she had gone quiet for a few years. It wasn't an angry silence – the occasional postcards he received seemed cheerful, detailing an energy healing practice in Baltimore; shifts on an organic dairy farm; an adopted husky that hated the Jacksonville heat; evening classes at Richmond Engineering. *Later, my alligator*, she wrote at the end of each postcard.

Then there had been the email. It had sat in his spam folder for twenty-four days, until, in desperation, waiting to hear back about a managerial job, he clicked into his junk folder to make sure he hadn't missed out on an offer.

If he had waited six more days, the message would have been deleted, and he could have had the bittersweet experience of not knowing what his mother's last words to him had been. He could have imagined a revocation of a hundred tiny hurts; an admission that the monkey was a phantom born of internalised guilt; a stand-in for an older sibling his conservative grandparents had forced up for adoption; or even that it never existed in the first place. At least – and above everything and all – that she had bigger regrets than him.

But her final email had been caught by his spam filter because it was just a forwarded link to a recipe for refried beans. Quite a good recipe, he had to admit, when he cooked it for Artur a few weeks later. The secret ingredient was bacon lard.

Rakhee wants to know about his father, straining to show post-coital interest after too many drinks at a book launch in Paris.

'And that's a whole other problem,' Marc says. 'You know, a normal person would be wondering about their father, daydreaming about some Latino guitar player or soccer star or even an extra from Cannibal Holocaust. *Hey, did you fuck a blonde American woman in 1978? But I don't, because it doesn't matter, when there's a damn monkey on my back.'*

Rakhee squints at him as she rolls a cigarette.

'Psychologically,' he adds, taking a drag and coughing.

In his mother's Roanoke house, Marc sorted through oceans of books, assorted gardening supplies, old editions of the *New Yorker*, a badly folded tent, three antique fur coats, an incomplete set of billiard balls, troupes of ceramic ornaments, and boxes and boxes of photographs.

In one box, he found faded Polaroids of his mother in the rainforest – long, loose hair; a swollen belly peeping out from under a cropped top; an ocelot cub at her feet, a parrot on her shoulder and a baby monkey slung around her hip – so that much of the story was true. But whether this was *the* monkey, he would never know.

In another photo, Kodak this time and yellow-hued, his middle-aged mother was holding up both hands, splayed out, with rings on each finger. *One for each lost love* was written on the back. Although considering her penchant for dramatics, it was as likely to be true that the rings were tin and glass, or were scavenged from an upturned gumball machine. None of the men in her life could be counted as loves, he considered, or even lost. More mislaid, like a useful but inessential trolley token.

At least the ones he knew about. There had been some men that she had cried over, and others who were chased out of the house, including, on one memorable occasion, a lover who escaped just ahead of the wild swings of a replica didgeridoo. A good-natured 'friend' had even lived with them in Barcelona for a year when Marc was thirteen. The man had painted his own fingernails blue at the kitchen table every Sunday morning, filling the house with the sharp scent of acetone. His mother had fancied herself a journalist that year and had disappeared for large chunks of time, always returning home with a token for him – a colourful bus ticket, an unfamiliar candy brand, a straw figurine.

Harlow

He forced himself to stop looking through the photographs after an hour. He couldn't understand how much of her was compressed into each one. They were angry, caged things, even though she was smiling in most of them.

On a roof in Lisbon, María-Rosa tells him to shut up, that she hates monkeys because their long fingers look like spoons. He can't argue with that, so he goes down on her instead, spelling out the alphabet with his tongue and stopping on the letters she likes best.

His mother couldn't remember the monkey's name. That's what annoyed him the most.

He found very little trace of himself while clearing the house in Roanoke, which made him feel equal parts wounded and smug. He revised and reworked what he would tell Artur when he was back in his bare London flat; how he would say it, what stance he would take, if he would let his eyes dampen or just lift his chin stoically in the face of such maternal neglect.

But then, in the kitchen, he came across a photograph of himself resting on the top of the fridge, blown up on a canvas frame as wide as his outstretched arm. He was about six, standing on a table, blowing a huge snot bubble out of his nostril while his mother lifted her fists in the background to cheer him on. She looked wild, ecstatic, with a mane of permed white-blonde hair, and he, in his checked shorts and baggy jumper, he looked like the king of the world. He had no memory of the scene, or of who might have taken the photograph, but the warmth of it almost singed his fingers. He stood on the canvas frame until it snapped under his weight, feeling like she had set these traps on purpose, raising a hidden stick each time he attempted to wallow in her neglect.

In a bar on the outskirts of Roanoke, a waitress gives him a free Old-Fashioned when he tells her that his mother has died. 'So sad, hun.' She pats him on the back. 'Try the buffalo sliders.'

He leaves her a large tip and waits half an hour, but she doesn't come to collect it.

On the evening of his second-last day in Virginia, he decided to finally tackle his mother's bedroom, a loft above the sitting room. He had intentionally left it for last, expecting a djinn's bottle of her thoughts and smells; one last chance for him to raise an emotion other than exasperation at her untidiness.

But the room was frustratingly bare. The wooden floorboards were splintering in places, and cobwebs infested the ceilings – as a child, Marc wasn't allowed to clear them for fear of disturbing the spiders, and had bashfully imported that habit to London – but besides that, the loft was tidy and stale.

Harlow

Her bed was neatly made on a raised stack of pallets, and the walls were grey stucco. A single lightbulb was looped around a beam in the rafters, which were low and heavy. A mirrored, full-length wardrobe sat in the furthest corner, and an uncomfortable-looking stool was arranged in front of a small window. On the roof outside, a bat box crouched under the eaves.

He sat down on his mother's stool as dusk settled on the room. From it, he could see for a short distance across the darkening city; over apartment blocks and factories and, on the horizon, the frosty peaking of the Blue Ridge Mountains. Traffic sounds filtered up through the still air, under the soft twilight flittering of bats setting out to hunt.

He stood up again after a few minutes, rubbing invisible dust off his hands, looking around the room for something to do; something, anything to dismantle and throw away. Finally, he heaved the mattress off the pallets and wrestled it through the door, letting it slide down the stairs like a bobsleigh. The exertion left him panting, but he felt slightly better.

He opened the door of the wardrobe and swung aside layers of bedsheets that hung like theatre curtains. In the back, there was a huddle of shapes and lines that caught in his fingers when he reached in to clear them. Something clanked and shifted in the dark. Marc stood back, sneezed a shower of dislodged dust into his elbow, and flicked on the dangling lamp.

how to gut a fish

He pulled the sheets aside again and the swaying light illuminated a set of jagged, gnashing jaws on a square metal head; a furred torso with limbs looped together on long, fine threads, still twitching at the elbows and knees where he had disturbed it. A stiff stick pierced the bottom of the mouth and made a hinge of the jaw, and a red felt tongue had been sewn into place. The terrible puppet had lightbulbs for eyes, with big red Xs instead of pupils, and a tail that curled up and around its own neck.

It was a crude, inelegant thing, cobbled together from tin cans, carpet swatches and lengths of wood, and he couldn't be sure that it wasn't an accidental arrangement, an optical illusion; that if he moved his head the angle of the light would change and the simian face would return to being a collection of trash and old strips of fabric.

A length of string dangled from the monkey's shoulders, and a piece of scruffy cardboard sat against its wire-hanger ribs. Marc stared at the piece of card, curled and aged at the corners. Then he began to laugh and laugh, startling a flurry of bats from under the eaves and out towards the mountains, because on the card was written his name.

dado

The air is sawdust, warm and dull, and the sweet smell of burnt timber licks up from under the buzz saw. The old school hall is high-ceilinged and echoing; thin metal chains drape from patchwork windows all the way to the concrete floor. A corridor wraps the main space like a curled intestine. In the bathrooms, the spit-hot rage of teenage girls lingers in black ink on the cubicle doors, and there are finely drawn scorch marks on the walls from a potassium toilet-bomb. The explosion had damaged the plumbing, just a little, but the excuse was enough to force the construction of new student prefabs further down the road, so a community centre has moved into the space.

A yoga class stretched here earlier; their purple mats have been piled in a far corner in loose, uneven rolls, like pursed lips against a windowpane. Yesterday, swing dancers chose partners from a wide, rotating circle and attempted the charleston for the third week in a row. Mondays, a cancer support circle; Fridays, a dwindling Scouts group, decimated by the early swirlings of puberty and a sci-fi programme that airs at the same time as the meetings. There has been talk among the parents of rescheduling, at least until the season ends, but there are no time slots free; and anyway, the troop leader says, a bend is as bad as a break, when it comes to children.

The builders come on Thursday evenings for two hours, but the time often flattens itself and distends further into the night. It is timetabled on the large whiteboard as a class, but there is no dividing line between tutors and students, just hands clutching plans and files and screwdrivers as if they are knots on an old rope. Metalworkers, wood-strippers, rewirers, rescuers, they work from instruction videos, their phones propped up against winter jackets, although the coverage is often patchy because of the thick concrete walls.

Two old schoolfriends, now middle-aged and soft-handed, are crafting a canoe, capturing memories of sparkling waves and salt-soaked skin to entomb in wood. An elderly man in paint-stained denims, boots that come up to his knees and claw marks of white hair across his forehead; he welds without a mask, but the sparks jack-knife away from his face. A woman, grey-haired since her twenties, is making a rocking horse, and each week she smooths away at the surface with fine sandpaper. A teenage asylum seeker comes along on foot and speaks gently; he makes nothing of his own, but carries and presses and measures for others. He smokes rolled-up cigarettes while he works and scatters paper skins like confetti. Around them, the thin September air drifts in under the half-open shutter and becomes warm, softening the whine of power tools and the twisting of clamps into a gentle purr.

Nine o'clock comes and goes; the projects are tidied away to one side of the hall to leave room for the next morning's art class, which will fill up the space with slashes of colours and sighs. The group disperses in fits and trickles, making shapes out of their hands to compare angles and lines laid down in steel and wood and rubber. On the way out, a conversation between the white-haired welder and the dislocated teenager dangles over the edge of familiarity with a question about plans for the weekend. But the conversation is salvaged and is drawn back to the solidity of a snapped drill piece.

Another man lingers behind them to fuss with an old credit card at a line of glue, teasing it, pushing each attempt at a drip back into the mass before it has a chance to stretch down on to the wood; if it spills, the trail will harden on the surface, and he will need to take a chisel to it. He is building a cabinet from plans downloaded on the lone, yellowed computer in the county library and printed for 15c per sheet. There will be four upper drawers and a cupboard below, but for now it is still skeletal, and he works slowly, so slowly; *measure twice, cut once*, he tells the others when they will listen.

When the glue finally begins to firm and hold, he is sated, rocking back on his heels and pushing his glasses up the bend of his nose. The building settles as he leaves, pulling the graffitied shutter down after himself. There is a wrist-thick chain and a padlock for the door, but it is rarely used; the community outcry and solidarity that a break-in would provoke would almost be worth the intrusion. Besides, the shutter is firm and heavy, and it makes a shuddering, solemn noise as it grazes and then settles on the concrete floor. The lamp above the entrance is motion acti-vated; it will startle a grazing rabbit twice in the early morning and light up once for no reason at all.

The man's dark-green Peugeot is in the furthest spot in the emptied car park, drawn up half on a pavement and half in thick grass. He had arrived late tonight, and the others were already head-bent and working by the time he came in. Headachy warmth from a moulding vanilla air freshener spills out as he opens the door, and his hands sink into the padded steering wheel. He slips into gear and out off the pavement, dipping his lights in salute as the old school hall falls away in his back mirror.

dado

The road home is narrow, but smooth; his mind sits with the cabinet he is making, exploring the hollow spaces that will be filled with drawers, shaping them with his fingers, counting the remaining sheets of panelling to be finished. Dried glue coats his fingers, and he worries at it with his teeth, pulling the skin off with the crust; the pink flesh burns a little at the first touch of air, but it will yellow and harden by morning.

The beams of the Peugeot's headlights gently churn, losing focus and breathing out into patches of autumn fog. A glow on the horizon brightens, splits into two and converges again. The man veers off the tarmac on to a swelling of grass, and waits for the other car to pass; the placement of the lay-bys as familiar as the knuckles on his hand. He closes his eyes as the passing light sears his face, then pulls out again. The driver-side window is half-open; the crisp air streams in across his forehead in a wide stripe while his ankles pool in warmth from the rickety heating system. He is thinking of drips; of hard, rounded shapes slipping from the wet glue and escaping down the smooth plywood, blurring the fine, sharp joints.

And then a distant splotch of canary-yellow swoops into focus and becomes a striped high-vis vest on a bicycle; screaming from the dark, filmy background to the foreground, and the car screams too, although the man's foot has already left the accelerator, screams as it rolls over rubber and spokes that break loose and stab at the heavy tyres, and air hisses and metal clatters in a dead and furious way, and he is rattled up and off his seat so hard his head hits the roof and slides sideways to stutter against the car-frame, and in his dazed fright his foot slams to the ground and the high-pitched, clanking sounds of twisted metal cough out once more and are left behind as he picks up whining, eager speed.

The road is still there, still somewhere, traced out in stop-motion as one shattered headlight flickers off and on, but it is memory alone that leads him home. Between his legs is a warm pool of urine, cooling rapidly and clinging to the dark hairs on the inside of his thighs, drying from the hot gusts panting out of the heater; the leather seat rejects the liquid, and it sits in the vee of his lap and washes from side to side against his groin as the car sways through the night and home.

In the morning, the red matchsticks on the clock-radio rearrange themselves and the news bells chime out. The man comes suddenly out of a drifting sleep that had crept in after an early-morning rousing, an hour vividly dream-stretched into a year. Groggy, he reaches over to the bedside table and fingers his smeared glasses, rubbing them against his belly through the creases of the salmon-coloured duvet.

He sleeps on a camp bed now; the old, queen-sized double mattress has been lifted and shoved up against the wall, trapped in place behind two full-length wardrobes, the bedframe dismantled. The lowness of the camp bed surprises him each morning, his feet jarring against the cold wooden floor like a slap, so he lies a little longer beneath the duvet, postponing the jolt of a new day. He thinks again of the fine, smooth lines of the cabinet, tracing its shape against the far bedroom wall for perspective, the single wall that is a garish, violent purple, because his wife had said it would perk them up in the mornings to see a colour so alive.

He had filled two metal skips with her things, but had kept the purple wall and an old recipe for *tamales* pinned to the fridge, brought home from a six-day Mexican holiday they had won in a crossword competition three years ago. They had walked for hours through Cancún in awe of their luck, stopping at stalls and little shops, eating *antojitos* until their fingers turned damp and shiny with grease. Ankles aching in evening restaurants, she had made lists and itineraries, and sulked when time refused to fit into her discrete packages. He had teased her about her Catalan-flavoured Spanish from a lost study year in Barcelona, and she had eaten a chilli pepper so hot she had stayed in the hotel bathroom for an hour while he watched *telenovelas*.

how to gut a fish

Her tumour had been discovered soon after in dizziness and stumbling, in words that came out sideways, and its spindly fingers had spread so far and so fast she was skin-stretched and wet-eyed in a month. He had clasped her hands between his knees at night, but she was whisked away in sunlight and daffodils, in an unseasonable April heatwave that had charmed green things from the earth in proud, thick tufts. Her passing had called home children and cousins and friends from far-flung corners; the church had been an overstuffed cushion, the funeral Mass spilling out into the road. His wife had the knowing of small kindnesses that braided tight bonds; a knowing that had frightened him at times.

At the airport, he had held his half-Australian granddaughter's hand in his for the first time. After the burial they had coloured together with thick markers while his grown-up son and daughter discussed his health, his schedule, his future, over endless cups of tea and triangle sandwiches. His granddaughter drew great, looping flowers and cats with exactly six whiskers; tree-strung houses billowing dark smoke; circle-handed figures with spaghetti hair. He added his own creations to the page: a lobster with the head of a rabbit had made her peal with laughter, and she had begged for more and more creatures, each christened with a name set down as solemnly as a vow. His children had spoken around him, as if the aching gap in him was vulgar, somehow, and they were wary of tumbling down and losing themselves in the weeds of his grief. But the little girl had rested her weight on him as they coloured, and had felt no fear at all.

His children had both left on the same weekend, and he had insisted on driving them to the regional airport, on hauling out a heavy black car seat for his granddaughter from the depths of a neighbour's garage. The little one had forgotten to wave goodbye, the casual cruelty of a child, and he had sat alone on the hard, grey seats of the departures lounge for a long, long time.

Early retirement from the post office came easily then, a decision made around him, a slippage rather than a leap. For a time, he tripped over cottage pies and banana bread set at his doorstep, clasped hands with passers-by in the street; found himself caught up in a weaving of old favours. But he has always been sharp-sided, and soon the fibres began to split beneath the awful denseness of his weight. Now he eats two boiled eggs for breakfast and takes brisk afternoon walks along the river, collects his weekly pension, waves and is waved to, but he is untethered and the days carry him along in their surf. His heart goes tick-tick, and sometimes tick-clank; he has pills to take to soothe its shivering. His body forgets to breathe in the night, ten heartbeats at a time, and he sits up gasping before turning over on the camp bed beneath the biting purple wall. He doesn't remember the wakenings.

This early in the morning, the headlines trickling down into the regional radio station are a day old, or detail some overnight move from Washington or the Middle East. Afterwards comes the national news and then the local, dribbled through the fingers of the guards and politicians: planning permission rows, notable social events, sports fixtures, break-ins and break-outs. Accidents, one nearly every morning: young and heartsore men slamming their feet against accelerators to doppler themselves out against tree trunks; bare, weeping car tyres slipping on patches of black ice; small hands slipping out of larger hands in brief, flashing moments that will be grasped after in dreams and wakefulness for years on end. And a torn high-vis vest, umbrellaed on the spokes of a bicycle wheel.

The morning newsreader finally talks herself into silence, ending awkwardly on an indrawn breath, and the presenter races to introduce a slow country song. But the breach of silence, the ugly, airy joint between the two voices, throbs through the room, across the salmon-coloured sheets, through the piles of newspapers, and presses itself up against the thick, frosted windows.

The talk of the hit-and-run is loud and strong as the news breaks across the community like the cresting of a dirty wave. There are pointed fingers and accusations, a criminal investigation ordered from above, angry letters from cyclists in the local paper, promises of cat's eyes on every road. The word about town is that the poor dead man had been a tourist; or a poacher; a delivery driver or a nurse – nobody is quite sure, although the woman in the flower shop says he was newly come to the area and had spoken to her once; he was impressed by the award-winning lilies she had nestled in an old fishing box outside her shop.

After the interviews and examinations, the cyclist's body is flown across the sea to elderly parents in the south German foothills. For a time, the accident is a dark, shapeless blot on drivers' windscreens as they pass along the route. Some bless themselves or tut, and others look away from the rotting, plastic-wrapped flowers left at the base of a nearby sycamore. A white cross is left one night under the bare branches of the tree. Nobody claims responsibility; crucifixes sprout like mushrooms along the verges.

At Halloween, parents think of the accident and, nervous of boy racers, confine their children to trick-or-treating along the pavements of their brightly lit housing estates. There is a well-attended firework display in a field on the outskirts of the town, and there are no reported firework injuries at the regional A & E for the first time in six years. The Scout troop organises a Monster Bash in the community centre. Prizes are awarded; the best pet category is won by a tan grey-hound with a stuffed jockey seated on its back. Around the snacks table, the topic of road safety is raised again.

A few locals begin a campaign for streetlights to extend further out from the heart of the town, to light up the back roads, and an online petition is started. It reaches over two thousand signatures when a campaigner does an angry interview on the local radio station comparing the allocated infrastructure funding to the aid sent overseas to an ongoing civil war in a small East African country. The matter is raised at a December county council meeting, and a preliminary plan is approved, but the funds are mired in an account for another six weeks due to an oversight by the secretary, whose mother hasn't been well. In his absence, he is quietly voted out of his position and the new secretary sets up a messaging group for internal discussions. Somebody paints IRELAND FOR THE IRISH on the back wall of the community centre and it is a number of weeks before a power hose is found to clean it off.

Just before Christmas, a young man is taken in for questioning about the accident; his blue Subaru is examined thoroughly and he is released. On New Year's Eve, he takes three tablets of Ecstasy and tells his friends that he has had enough; that he did hit the stupid cunt, reversed over him too; that he couldn't give two shits for him or for the whole fucking lot of them any more. He sets off for a construction job in the city, leaving his car to rust in his mother's back garden. In a pique of frustration, she offers to sell it in January to a local mechanic. The mechanic hums and haws for a few days, then buys it off her for less than it is worth. When the adrenaline subsides, she calls her son to tell him, and he swears to kill her with a baseball bat, leaving her in tears.

The village council meets again in the new year, and instead of funding the streetlights, the money is assigned to a cattle grate at the base of the bridge that crosses the river, because two lambs and a nursing mother had fallen into the water the previous weekend and drowned. In the messaging group, somebody sends around an all-caps chain message warning of data theft; another sends an off-colour cartoon.

The cyclist's mother flies over from Munich in early February for the inquest and sits quietly in the back of the high-roofed room while strangers make statements of fact about her son. Afterwards, she rattles her way down from the city on the cheapest bus to see the spot where the accident happened, but the back roads are nameless and the sycamore tree has no leaves left to identify it. She buys vinegar-sodden chips from the smaller of the two Chinese takeaways for the bus journey back. Her hips ache against the shallow commuter seats but the warmth of them throbs in time with her low and quiet rage.

how to gut a fish

The angle of the evening sun dusting the floor of the community centre has slightly changed; winter has dragged and released. The yoga mats are still piled in an uneven purple heap, and the sweat from yesterday's swing dancing class lingers in the air like oil on water. But the high windows have been cleaned and a capsule coffee machine has appeared, sponsored by a poorly attended table quiz; mugs fuzz and steep in the sink of the kitchenette. Space heaters plink in exhausted relief in the first sunlit evening of spring.

The Thursday group filters in, taking up their tools and speaking softly, as if moving an overfull jug across a narrow bridge. Fixer-uppers, refurbishers, builders, rescuers, their numbers have swelled, slightly, by a handful of newcomers, including the mechanic, who stopped in one evening for a look and has found himself returning weekly to dispense advice on faulty connections and steady wiring. But the ancient welder has been admitted to a care home after a suspected stroke, and the teenage asylum seeker stepped out for a call early one December evening and has not come back. The grey-haired woman still sandpapers her rocking horse. The canoe is now finished and has been painted a brilliant, liquid green with the help of the art class and a local sponsor, and the launch will take place the first weekend of May. The town's councilman will be there, to shake hands and talk about community values; he will sit in the boat for a photograph and smile for a second or two longer than is necessary. Other projects have more bones or a metal ribcage, and a couple have added flesh and electric veins, but most linger on, unfinished, as a safe anchorage in the lapping circles of conversation.

The green Peugeot comes late, and limps into the spot furthest away from the building. The mechanic, seeing it awkwardly parked, offers to have a look at the broken headlight, but the driver seems surprised when the damage is pointed out. He tells the mechanic that he doesn't drive at night these days, and besides, the car, no more than himself, is an old dog that has had its day.

The man moves through the building, nodding at nobody in particular, and finds the corner where he stores his cabinet. It now has one completed drawer and a frame that is fully backed in plywood. The man has decided that hardwood knobs will make a pleasing accent against the lighter grain, so he is smoothing at lumps bitten from a slab of old, dark mahogany. He takes up his hand-plane and the skin on his upper knuckles becomes reddened as he works.

He sees the cabinet finished, painted a sky blue, filled with little dresses and white socks. He sees it covered with stickers; unicorns and flowers and glow-in-the-dark stars.

lemons

High-flung handfuls of white polystyrene shapes, falling in gentle waves.

A package has come early for Christmas, and the two children have stolen away the S-shaped filling to make snow showers in their small, street-facing garden. Leaping into the air from balled toes, they catch pieces in their mouths, biting down so hard their teeth meet in the middle and slip to the side with a dry, squeaking noise. The taller girl spits a chunk of soft plastic out, and the other copies her in echoing delight. With it comes a smear of blood; a loose milk tooth has left a pinkish trail across the surface. She begins to cry, in fright, and panic fills up her eyes.

The older one laughs at the sight of the blood; she is eight years old and afraid of nothing, fierce as the sun. A thick headband scrapes her hair back against her skull, and she is barefoot through the cold grass, weaving around the thistles stippling the cramped front lawn of their terraced house. Her sister's brief terror subsides, and they resume their dance. They are whirling together in a snow globe, and they must catch each piece of polystyrene and launch it skywards again; if all the pieces fall to the earth at once, they will become figurines, frozen in place forever.

Across the road, a wet-lipped man leans against a grey cement windowsill and watches the handfuls of soft foam float down. His right hand is hidden in his dark jeans. He has cut a hole in the scooped lining of his pocket so he can grab himself through it, to pull and pull and pull.

The girls look up as one, sparrow-like, to see him staring. The older one becomes suddenly uncertain, unsettled by the man's jerking motions; a marionette moving without strings. They run inside, hand in hand, and the last of the polystyrene settles down on the lawn to wait for the wind to carry it off and up against the chain-link fence.

———

The girl is thirteen, and her teeth are chattering, like they do in cheerful adventure stories, but it is a painful, jumping thing and her jaw hurts from the strain. The sun has lashed whip-cracks of red across her back where her mother's suncream-coated hands had missed, but the ocean had been cold, so cold the shock of it had stunned her, and it had taken the scraping of a foot against a line of needled rocks to shock her back into breathing again. A blonde-haired girl, a friend so new the thread between them remains spiderweb thin, had jumped in straight after her, almost on top of her head, and they had been pulled under into a swirling, grey-green crypt.

Now they are shivering in the single shower cubicle together; clinging to each other in a giggling, salty mess. The blonde girl rubs her sanded hands up and down her own body, pulling her swimming togs away from her chest with an elastic snap. For a second, her soft, rounded breast is on display; a puppy-fat nipple the colour of strawberry lollipops.

The shower is only warm compared to their chilled skin, and as they thaw they begin to shiver again, so they rub themselves dry with rough, over-washed towels before throwing on sweat-damp clothes. They walk from the beach to the shop to buy chocolate cigarettes, eating them in nibbles, paper and all. They share a dip-bag of orange sherbet between them, and the grittiness coats their lips.

Later, as the girl cycles her bike home alone, her salted togs wrapped in a towel and lodged in her armpit, she will think of the nipple, wet-sleek and smooth as a pencil-top eraser.

how to gut a fish

Just like a period, but heavier than usual, the instructions had said, in fractured English, but the cramps are coming faster and harder, so she is pressed against the side of the bath, the chill of the porcelain nibbling at the edges of pain. The room spins unfairly, shuddering up and down, and closing her eyes makes the feeling worse, so she stares at the wall, counting the tiles from the top to bottom, making sure the diamond pattern repeats cleanly.

The pills had sat in her mouth for too long, turning her spit thick and choking and bitter, and the memory of the oval outlines remains under her tongue. They had arrived in an anonymous package from France, wrapped up with a silken scarf and some almond sweets that had been stale as soon as they came out of the box. The sender, a disapproving cousin, a pharmacist, hadn't added a postcard or note, and she had suspected the tablets were fake; a blast of B12, or a dose of iron to combat pregnancy-related anaemia. But now she can finally, finally feel the movement inside her, and she raps her forehead against the rim of the bathtub in gratitude, once, twice, and again.

The whine of the Smashing Pumpkins seeps in; her housemate is listening to music as he works on his final thesis corrections. She is annoyed by the intrusion into this private, sealed-off capsule of pain. The music is drawing lines from her emptying womb to a cassette player in the next room, across the sea to an American singer with a razor in his throat, and all the way back to this flat, this bathroom, this tiled floor.

The pain crests again, in anger.

The clumping will be lemon-sized, she has heard, but this is too strange for her to understand. Lemons are tart and firm, waxy and unyielding; joyful exclamation marks that are too bright, too yellow for this comparison. Her teeth clamp into the fleshy part between thumb and wrist, hard enough to dent, the outline of each tooth individually carved.

The singer hits a high note, a belly-song of hurt, and then there is a final wetness, a pulling from deep inside, and the pain comes stronger and truer than ever.

———

She is a woman and her little sister is twenty-two, drunk, and sobbing; wet, clunking things that come up from the diaphragm in retches to spill out over the lips. They are sitting on her couch, leather-backed and specially made to fit the angled walls of her newly bought apartment.

A row of half-drunk cups of tea move from hot to warm to cool along the table, and she taps them gently with a teaspoon while she waits for a pause in the flood, each singing out a different note, a song that is bright and pure. The cups are white china, a housewarming gift from an elderly aunt, and usually live on a shelf above the microwave, with chunkier supermarket mugs for everyday use. But the night-time knock on the door, the sour, nostril-burning tang of vomit; this moment requires more help than those mugs can provide, so the china has been laid out, to fill up with heartache.

Her sister's head comes up from its hollow in her lap and falls backward against the arm of the couch, her neck a convex curve of misery. Her upper lip shines with mucous, and a silvery trail dances along the backs of her hands, up the black sleeves of her knitted jumper.

The telling is not easy – a party, a couch, a drink – the words that come out are put together wrong, the sentences fall apart, and tears overwhelm meaning. So she smooths her sister's hair down again and again, but the red dye has made it rough and sticky, so it is an uneasy thing, like stroking a cat backwards.

It is so late it has become early, and the woman has work in the morning – a performance review – but the contract between sisters is old and stronger than sleep. The woman begins to hum, and a soothing, careful song fills up the room with layers of softness, until calm descends like a parachute.

---

lemons

Clara is almost two, all soft edges and pudge, and she is sleeping, making wet, rumbling noises in her white pine cot. The woman's daughter is named after the sick girl in *Heidi*, and her first, halting steps last week had truly seemed those of an invalid escaping a wheelchair. The Victorian sicknesses of her childhood books had always seemed curable through laughter and fresh air and green things, but her daughter's lungs are weak, so she wraps her in two jumpers and a jacket for visits to the playground, and carries hand sanitiser in her bag at all times.

The bars in the cot have been raised higher, because Clara had somehow managed to scale them the night before. She had bum-shuffled her way into the bedroom, pulling herself upright at the end of the bed, to see why Mam and Dad were fighting, moaning, banging into each other with exhausted passion. An unclaimed leg had arced out to catch their daughter across the cheek, and the cry of shock had caused her boyfriend to lose focus and ejaculate. They had both leaped up, sticky and dripping, scooping up their daughter in warm hands, shouting at each other in wordless, mindless guilt.

The baby sleeps well, now, and the high jail bars of her cot do not bother her, but her eye socket is yellow-dark and bruised. A puddle of shame lies in the centre of their double bed, and the surprised shrieks of pain will echo through the bedroom for months. At night, they still hold hands, but turn their backs to sleep.

how to gut a fish

The fresh teeth marks are dark smudges on her daughter's neck, but she wears them with satisfaction, hair slick-stiff with last night's hairspray. Clara is fifteen and her breath is still sugary sweet from alcopops and stolen cigarettes; eyes like spittle, she is vibrating at a black-and-red frequency as she sits at the kitchen table, sipping from a pint of water.

It is mid-morning, and her daughter's key had shuddered in the lock just an hour before. The woman is making an omelette for Ben before his football practice, but the effort of ignoring her daughter is limescaling the walls. Ben, oblivious, flicks brightly coloured questions at his older sister, and she bats them back across the room with morning-after wit. There will be screaming and accusations later, when her husband returns, but for now, a quiet fury splays itself out across the table like a dog in heat, throbbing and raw.

When Ben leaves to gather his football socks, she hands her daughter a silver dessert spoon and tells her to press the cold bowl against her neck until it begins to hurt, to soften the outline of the hickeys. Close up, her daughter smells foreign, the way other people's houses smell wrong, and her eyes leak a giddy mixture of resentment and pride. She cries softly after Clara stumbles to bed at lunchtime, cries as she plates the leftover omelette on to a separate dish, cries as she scrubs baked-on egg from the curved rims of the heavy-based frying pan.

The heat comes on the woman at night, mostly, but her sweat-soaked body begins to cool almost as soon as she gasps herself awake. She grips the duvet, easing it away from her sleeping husband, until the roaring in her ears subsides, and the sounds of the house slip back in.

Ben is awake and moving down in the kitchen, but she resists the urge to go to him. Her son spends the day in online games and virtual reality and ghosts around the house at night, and enough trust to leave him alone does not come easily to her. The new medication drives him to eat, and she finds loaves of bread half-spilled on the counter in the morning, butter-stained knives balanced on the edge of the sink. He has put on weight; his belly flops outwards over his jeans, but he refuses to leave the house long enough to buy a new pair. Clara doesn't understand his worries, his dark times, his scratchings at the wall; she calls her younger brother a waste of space when she visits home at weekends.

But mothers are burdened with second sight; she sees the terror behind his eyes and knows he would gnaw off his own leg to be free of it. She has her own terror, too: he will be learning to drive next year and her nightmares are of dark metal shapes twisted around roadside oaks. With the terror comes anger, when her womb pumps rage straight into her veins in a last, dying convulsion, and she is filled up with a muted, foggy fury that cannot find a target.

She should find her slippers, go downstairs to speak to Ben, hear his hurts; show her body that motherhood is not so easily thrown off. But instead, she lies in bed until dawn glows on the horizon, and the flushes of warmth pulse through her body every few minutes, like a great, beating heart.

———

The smooth place beneath her collarbone where her left breast used to be takes up space in the woman's mind, but it is negative space, like a scoop removed from an ice-cream tub. It doesn't bother her any more, really, and her husband kisses her there when he remembers to, or when he sees her tracing a circle around her upper ribs in the mirror. But now the other breast is pulsing too, the poison is heavy and angry; her lymph nodes have jumped into the fray. She fingers it, testing the weight, trying to decide if healthy tissue feels heavier or lighter, and fatigue drips down from her shoulders to spread like honey across the tiled kitchen floor.

She has seen an image online of a row of lemons, all lumpy and pockmarked, each darkened with a different malformation. *Spot the signs of cancer*, the caption had said, but sometimes signs are unnecessary, and knowing comes as easily and suddenly as the breaking of the day. Her husband also knows, or thinks he knows, because he sits up late most nights with his laptop and files, but the arrangement of paper never changes, because he stares at the wall instead of working and comes to bed benzo-drenched and snoring.

Clara is in Vancouver, too pregnant to fly; Ben sits in university in Dundee, racing through final accounting exams the woman wouldn't let him skip. But her sister is coming to visit soon, and they will drink tea out of their aunt's china cups and cry and talk about the future, or lack of. She will not say things about unfairness, or stolen time; her sister is pragmatic and knows that things are how they are, and will be as they will be.

The smart lighting changes automatically as the sun goes down, and the room turns buttery-soft, like the gentlest of sunsets. The woman can see herself in the darkened windows; her reflection floats on the surface as if a sharp knife could peel it free.

A digital chime calls out as the sliding door pulls across, and a red-dyed head pokes through, bringing with it a lick of December wind. She turns away from the sound and cocks her head to one side as her sister scrapes her boots against the doorframe.

Polystyrene snow, she says, as if resuming a long-interrupted conversation, *do you remember the polystyrene snow?*

cautery

Two accidents had framed most of Anna's grandfather's life, and in between there had been some living. The first, at the age of fifteen, had seen him tangled in the drivebelt of a threshing machine. Only for a second or two, before his brother pulled him out, but it was enough to twist his spinal cord, but gently, like the kneading of a cat.

His mother had watched the accident happen, looking over the lower fields from the farmhouse window, and had fallen to the floor in a faint. She had lived with a terrible fear of machines since witnessing a tractor overturning on a bridge as a child, and this had set some mental countdown to disaster ticking. While her elder son had worked to stem his brother's bleeding, she had stood up and calmly flagged down a passing neighbour to request he send the undertaker along. The neighbour had heard the very-much-alive roars from the field and had instead sent the doctor, and the mother had seemed only faintly surprised when she was told her younger son would live.

Oh, she had said, *oh!* the first quiet and low, and the second louder, as if recognising an old friend.

After the first accident, Anna's grandfather had been left with a slump down the left side of his body. Not a full paralysis, just a slowness, or a misunderstanding, as if his brain were speaking a different language, one that he had known a long time ago in a dream. He had certain spots of complete numbness that would worsen and spread when he was tired, and a disobedient elbow that sometimes jerked straight as a rod, flinging whatever he was holding off at a right angle.

The second accident had come almost fifty years later, the gap having been filled with a cautious flirtation, a speedy, white-bumped marriage, three sons, a daughter, a few rounds of sickness in his cattle, a few more fields, a few less fields, and the death of his mother and brother.

He had been perched on his tractor in an autumn pasture, watching cattle pick at a fresh load of silage, when he took his bog-oak pipe out to light it. His wife hated the smell of it and wouldn't let it in the house, even now that the children were all grown, but he still found that pockets of quiet felt better with the curl of tobacco in the air. The pipe had grown warm in his hand as the sun dipped lower, marking the animals with flat, slanting light. He tapped the wooden stem against the side of his seat to clear it, and an ember slipped from the bowl down and into the cuff of his trousers, where it proceeded to burn a hole through the fabric, the skin, the meat of his calf, and out the other side. The numbness that had settled on his body at the age of fifteen kept him from noticing, until a sudden whiff of roasting meat had nudged his stomach awake. All the way home he had entertained the idea of charred pork for dinner, with green orchard apples on the side, and it was only when he stepped off his tractor seat and the leg collapsed under him that the problem was discovered.

Years later, he told his other grandchildren that it was a bullet wound, gained fighting off an armed intruder, or two, or five, with a shotgun, or pitchfork, depending on the telling, and a set of gardening shears if he was in a particularly silly mood. But to Anna he told the truth, one day, because he checked her little open mouth and announced that she had an uncrooked tongue, which meant she had no space in her for lies.

While a horde of uncles and cousins watched a football match in the big front room, her grandfather showed her the coin-sized hole in his calf. By that stage he was in a wheelchair, reassigned to a new extension off the back of the farmhouse with the bed on the same level as the bathroom. Bending had become difficult for him, so Anna had rolled down his sock for him with her six-year-old hands, feeling the shining, hairless patch where the cuff of his boots had worn the skin bald over the years. He smelled of sweet metal and the warm, sleeping scent of a dog.

She knelt on the hard, tiled floor, pressing her chubbed fingers against the bone of his shin. The hole was clean, instantly cauterised as it had been, but the sagging skin around it felt to her like a drawing of a raincloud. She leaned lower and looked into it, closing one eye and then the other, as if it were a telescope, then pressed her longest finger through the hole and out the other side. *How does it feel?* she asked her grandfather, and he thumbed her freshly pierced ears with a wink of comparison.

Soon after that, a year or so, or maybe only a few weeks – the time seemed to stretch and flex like an accordion in her memory – a heart attack had finished off what the drivebelt had started. Anna couldn't remember his funeral, although she could pick out her own pale, rounded face amongst a shower of cousins in a group photograph taken on the front lawn. Her grandfather's little terrier could be seen off in a corner rolling in something dark and foul, but her parents had framed the image nonetheless.

When she was first asked by an adult what she was going to be, Anna said she already was. The room had been full of second cousins and neighbours; her

mother had wanted to celebrate the arrival of her baby
brother Misha into the world with a bang, and had
sent the party invites far and wide. Anna's response,
so quick and sure, had set her least-favourite uncle
to laughing, the one with the wet lips and cold, cold
hands. He had called a hush on the room to repeat
her words and tugged on her ponytail as he spoke.
She escaped to the hot press and cried sharp tears
of rage for her absent grandfather, and a full hour of
muffled noise and celebration passed before her father
found her to offer a plate of dessert; a berry pavlova so
crisp it hurt her tongue.

The next time Anna was asked what she was going
to be, she said she wanted to be a librarian. Her mother
was a teacher and her father a farmer like his father, so
the list of jobs she felt she could pick from was limited.
Not a teacher; already the boldness of the boys in her
primary-school class infuriated her. And the spittle
and sweat of animals frightened and then disgusted
her; she had swapped bedrooms with Misha so her
window overlooked the road rather than the field. As
a last resort, her hopeful father had called her to watch
a calving, and she had dreamed for weeks that she was
wrapped, drowning, in the red meniscus of birth.

But in the county library, she loved to watch the
calm, auburn-haired librarian fade up and down the
aisles, her silent presence enough to quiet giggling
teenagers in the Mills & Boon section, her pockets

filled with stickers for sulking children. She had a cat's secret smile that only revealed itself when she unearthed a particularly hard-to-find novel. The coloured labels marking the spine of every book fascinated Anna, and whenever she found a yellow amongst blues, or a grey with greens, she would move the book to the correct section and feel a pleasantly tight sensation at the bottom of her ribcage, like she was wearing an invisible seatbelt.

She was to be a librarian for a few more years, but when, in her final term of secondary school, she had sat for a long time in a high-ceilinged room and answered questions about spatial awareness, the relationship of one thing to another, and the dancing of angles and numbers, the answer spat out by the machine had been a jumbled horoscope. *Practical, systematic, detached*: the arrogance of the words had made her want to scratch holes in the reflective screen of the computer. *Law*, suggested her career guidance counsellor, and there had been enough of a media trend towards gritty courtroom dramas that she had applied for it without too much of an argument; most of her time had been taken up with being tired, in any case.

Her younger brother Misha contracted echolalia around this time and became insufferable, following her from room to room, repeating her own words back to her, but changing the inflection slightly, which was more annoying than the repetition. He also refused to take his runners off indoors, claiming that the static from the carpets could cause spontaneous human combustion, having read about it in an old *Reader's Digest* in the attic. The article had sat alongside a black and white picture of a woman's foot in a low patent heel, severed at the ankle, surrounded by a pile of ashes.

In her second year of a law degree, Anna found that one of the coursebooks assigned in her tort module was missing a chapter. It had been snipped out precisely at the roots and the remains of the pages stuck out obscenely like a blunt fringe. In the dim light of the library, she ran her thumb along the tufts of paper to feel the soft spaces where the words had been. *The others are competitive all right*, the librarian had said, when Anna presented the book to her, tapping at her computer with one hand, her arm stretched far from the keyboard like a character in the background of a film scene. *Tough luck*, she added, when Anna remained standing at her desk.

It was only when the electronic barriers at the exit to the library beeped in protest that Anna realised she was still cradling the book in her arms like a wounded infant. The security guard was just beginning to rise from his desk when she flung it at his feet and ran through the barrier again. *These students are fucking mental*, he said, loud enough to startle two American tourists who were peering through the large library windows. The building was a monstrous steamer ship, lattices of yellow windows blinking off as desk lamps were retired for the evening.

When she walked out of her final exams, Anna had the sensation of being on a conveyer belt, one that had suddenly stopped and left her unbalanced. That night, in the dying stages of a house party, she slept with someone for the first time; a friend of a friend who rolled over as soon as he had finished and began to read articles on his phone. Anna had been ashamed of her dryness and pulled her black tights up over her knees underneath the covers, returning downstairs with the bend of them still constricting her legs. She sat for a while in the ashy circle of conversation, but after a time she decided that every story being told in that room was a variation on her own life. Her partner didn't reappear downstairs, so she went to the bathroom without looking in the mirror and slipped out the back door while the others roared at a video of extreme animal attacks set to a cheerful soundtrack. The blue-black hickeys the other student left on her neck lasted for an entire week, delaying her return home for fear Misha would pull at her skin and query them.

She completed two weeks of her traineeship in family law before she left. The barrister she was assigned to shadow, an older man with black hair streaking from his nose, had pressed an armload of files into her grasp in the lobby of the courthouse and sent her up three flights of stairs; when she reached the top, he was already there ahead of her and tapped her shoulder conspiratorially. *Always ask if there's a lift*, he said, as if this was some worldly maxim meant to awe her.

The barrister's custody cases that day were all adjourned, some for reasons of illness or misunderstanding, but others for the sake of an early lunch. Anna fumed the whole way back home, seated on the floor of a train carriage, carrying her black patent loafers in her hands. Eventually, as the train emptied, she noticed that one of her solicitor's clients was sharing the same carriage; a thin, sweating man in his forties who, earlier that day, had asked her where the bathrooms in the courthouse were, although she had got the feeling that he already knew.

As they moved out and away from the city, the seat opposite him freed up and Anna slid into it, flicking through the yellow sheets of maintenance applications in her lap until she found the file belonging to the client and began to read. The train rattled on into the night and soon they were the only people left, and the red heat of the harsh words began to blur and bicker on the page. She finished reading about the case and tried to glare at the man opposite, but he wouldn't look at her, resting his long sleeves on the table, smelling of dampness and rage.

how to gut a fish

She watched his reflection in the chill, dark window as he worked his way through six small bottles of red wine from the trolley. He popped the plastic skirt off the final bottleneck and stuck his tongue through the hard, black opening. It creased and twisted as he wiggled it over and back; she could see the red throb of his tastebuds through the plastic ring. His eyes swung to meet the eyes of her own reflection and she let her pupils relax, but still, she could hear the squelch and click of his tongue excavating the hole. She knew that he was laughing at her.

Emile took her out for dinner the evening before she left for Spain. Her friend had orange hair that she dyed a deeper red with henna imported from India, and freckles that she darkened with a brown pencil eyeliner. They had met in a shared History of Law lecture; Emile went on to have a minor breakdown and was hospitalised for a month before dropping out of her Classics degree. Anna had liked her better before it and would have been happy to drift apart, but Emile seemed to cling to their annual meetings like handholds on a climbing wall. She was jealous, she said, jealous of Anna's guts, jealous that she was the one going off on her own to teach English in Spain, although in truth it would have taken a winkling knife to pry Emile out of her boyfriend's two-storey apartment.

Are you worried? she asked, pressing her lips together in wide-eyed concern. Anna considered this as the waiter cleared away their platters. Her secondary-school Spanish was rusty, but the school assured her it wouldn't be a problem. Her father was unhappy that she had quit the traineeship, it was true, although her mother was a great believer in finding oneself, never considering that Anna's goal was more to lose everyone else. Misha was in a difficult phase again, but he hadn't seemed to mind that she was leaving, although as she passed his bedroom one night, he had called her into the darkness to warn her to watch out for *el Cuco*, the ghost of a man who drank the blood of children to cure his tuberculosis.

As the restaurant lights dimmed and the flames of somebody else's birthday cake swayed across the room, Anna decided that she had never really been worried about anything in her life – anxious, stressed, sad, nervous, yes – but worry seemed an abstract thing, undefined and untethered; the opposite of an emotion.

On her first day of teaching in the dry Mediterranean air, the students noticed her sweaty face and the wet stain between her breasts, although the shirt's label had claimed it to be lightweight and breathable. Two teenage girls fanned her with their magazines, while a third had torn Anna's hair tie out and reassembled her sweat-lank hair into a tight braid, which was, they assured her in Spanish, much better suited to the heat. Her face coloured with embarrassment, but afterwards, she began to understand that the shame of perspiration was unknown here in the open summer, where it was as inevitable as the dawn.

The classroom had metal bars across the window instead of glass to keep the room cool. The breeze was welcome, but the noise that spilled out from other classrooms meant that teaching had to be confined to a small space around the whiteboard. Only those students that were interested would scooch their chairs forward to hear her, and her voice often cracked in the dry air.

For her first few weeks, she had taught her meticulously planned lessons clearly, if tentatively, but it seemed all her students were speaking just a little too loud. They were teenagers, after all, and to have them speaking English at all was an achievement, a science teacher told her, even if Anna had to ignore the crude and thinly veiled description of her vagina that one hulking sixteen-year-old submitted as classwork. She gave him a seven out of ten for his descriptive language; circling the words *luscious* and *moist* as good use of vocabulary.

cautery

In a villa on the outskirts of the small rural town where she was staying, her elderly landlady spoke to her of Franco's War, how her mother had been killed by an air strike while queuing at the central market for fish, how *agua roja* from the rubble had run down the street like blood. In Anna's bedroom, a foot-high statue of Jesus Christ on the cross was kept under a bell jar; his face contorted with agony, the heads of nails emerging from his feet and palms. The statue was unpainted, but his heart, his heart sat red and pulsing on his chest, twined with thorns and leaves. She sent a postcard to Misha describing the grisly figure, but he did not reply, and it was only later that she realised she had forgotten to include a return address.

The day the cicadas woke, Anna thought some ancient flock of birds had been startled; or an industrial sawmill had started up on a distant hill; or an air-raid siren was signalling the return of the bombers. Hands over her ears, she walked into the classroom to find her students unfazed, playing *juego de la lapicera* at the back of the room, leafing through tabloids filled with glossy-pored celebrities, and pumping music through a small, portable speaker. They were puzzled by her distress, until one finally opened his mouth in an O of understanding, and a barrage of Spanish flooded out.

how to gut a fish

Chicharra!

Fly, they explained, flapping arms above their heads.

Insect, offered Luis, the boy who had described her genitals with such care.

Finally, a girl pulled up an image on her phone, showing a fat, oil-slicked insect with veined wings. Anna stared at the alien thing and imagined the crunch of it under her strapped leather sandals, in between the base of her palms, and between her teeth.

At the end of the day, Luis was waiting for her in the car park, leaning against a peach-coloured wall with huge headphones covering his ears. It was after four at that point, and the few remaining cars belonged to teachers marking papers, bar one or two owned by the security guard and the maintenance workers.

Anna sensed his hunched shape out of the corner of her eye, but she didn't look at him, instead wiping her hands on her long skirt and checking her bag for a set of essays. She ignored him to walk towards the chain-linked fence where her bicycle was locked, but he reached for her wrist as she passed. She pulled her hand from his grip and looked into his coffee-stained eyes as the cicadas droned on and on and on.

Luis took her hand again, firmer this time, and she let him lead her away from the building, up and over a small series of hummocks, across a creek. The whine of noise was so thick she felt she was wading through chest-high water. Around the back of the school, beyond the football pitch, there was a dusty field lined with carob trees, their hard, half-moon pods littering the ground. The sun was still high and the warmth of the day was pooling, becoming concentrated in a last push before evening. Her head felt tight; her braid seemed to pull every hair at once and each one she tried to pluck from the weaving set another two burning, like her skull was a ball of wet elastic bands.

Aquí, aquí, the boy muttered to himself, letting go of her wrist and veering to the right, into a small hollow. He began to scratch at the dry earth like a bloodhound. Anna lifted her eyes to the white-streaked sky, shading them with her hand, staring until the duck-egg blue became dotted with flashing smudges of navy. The buzzing softened to her ears after a few minutes, but every now and then the volume would rise again, a physical thing, like a swelling in the back of her throat.

Luis finally looked up at her, urgently beckoning. *Aquí, aquí,* he repeated, *los chicharras vienen.*

There was a cluster of indentations in the ground, perfectly circular, with ridges of dust thrown up around the edges, as if the earth was a stretched-out sheet that had been stabbed with a hot poker. Anna dropped to her knees to look closer. Emerging from one of the holes was a white nymph the size of her index finger, red-orange eyes burning against a pale, mud-smeared body. The insect's wings were tucked back, and segmented limbs flicked out like fingers shaking off drops of water. It crawled slowly forward, as if convinced of something.

Anna's skirt fell forward as she leaned in to stare at the circular marks in the soil, and her calves were bare to the sun. She saw again the hole burned in her grandfather's leg, the feel of it pressed against her eye socket, the wrinkled edges of skin that framed what she could see through it: the black sock on his other leg, the metal of the wheelchair, a short length of corridor dotted with other ankles, and his ancient terrier, squatting low over an unguarded plate of food. The perforations in the earth became cloud-edged and multiplied, repeating again and again into an intricate pattern, a pattern so deep and vast the soil itself began to sag and fall apart.

Luis's hand moved to the place where her thigh met her knee and settled there. All around her, the cicadas sang and sang, collapsing in on themselves and reinflating, chests whining with the monstrous roar of summertime. The boy's hand was cool against her skin, which, unguarded from the afternoon sun, was turning warm and pink. As another nymph poked its head out from a hole, like the tip of a boil, she sat back on her haunches, trapping his fingers beneath the weight of her thigh, and felt her sweat begin to pool in that soft grove of skin.

mantis

Dawn colours like dusk but turned inside out. Head is banging but need to find green rooftop cross where is it? City waking up now and black lines of buildings squeezing together into train tracks. Shadows falling down hard metal poles. My eyes so dry do two hard blinks. But not full wet-black just little fireworks pink and orange flashes. Sharp tears my eyes. In the air pollen powder shaking from tree branches. Only spring but too warm for it maybe summer flowers all confused so popping off early. Or just smoke in air tiny bits of dirt wrapped into clouds like shit on wool. Smell it too up my nose and all over. Shit on street shit in eyes shit raining from the sky there's a poem a bedtime story for our boy Ellen—

too early for pharmacy other shops only opening but my boy needs drugs his wheeze is bigger than him. Scares the crap out of me with the dry hack of it. His breath like roll of thread unwinding. Little hands clawing it back into himself stuffing it down into lungs
structures called bronchioles shaped like

cauliflower the nurse described them thought she was being funny but then he was up in the night wailing nightmares cauliflower in his chest

don't even like it Da it goes all bitty and crumby tastes like tissues Da don't want it in me

what a bint of a doctor too. Cold hands hair scraped back into topknot like bread roll. Flicking pen filling out forms yes this this and this. My ears trying to listen take it in. Our boy pushing trucks around on the floor not a bother on him but the hack of it the dry wheeze of it. Nasal spray corticosteroids inhalers too brown to prevent purple to maintain and blue to relieve. What a rainbow what a rainbow to be giving a child and the price the price of it Ellen you know—

my feet still swollen throbbing red and black and red and black in time with banging head. Need just a drop of water the thirst in me my dry mouth rough tongue like cat. Concrete still dark from early rain air all thick with it. Not cat tongue more like whale with big net of a mouth like one in documentary with posh man reading his voice soft like fresh tobacco

the baleen whale uses filter feeding to isolate krill and

need to suck in damp air filter out tiny pieces of wet because the thirst on me. Pharmacy here now ahead here we go here we go! But shutters down still closed fuck go further down the hill into town. Your fault Ellen if it takes a while you won't let me in the house won't let me wake up next to you say

mantis

I need space to think

but space won't change naught. Bet another lad taking up the space filling up your cunt sucking on your tits Ellen forgotten me already

no

reel thoughts back and straighten out head. Just your shape alone in dark room arched bare back covers kicked off. Gritty eyes because of the hack of him all night the dry hack of our boy. And then dawn comes and my phone blips

bad night get cough bottle

and then afterwards

pink one

wouldn't say that to just anyone would *explain* would *ask*. But just five words then two enough for me now you couldn't say that to a tit-sucker Ellen could you—

my head shrivelling up like walnut such throb. Brown creases and pink lumps tiny channels for thoughts all dried out. Little sip of water before I left Kev's but not too much the fear of it pain in the kidneys and pissing fire. Had to sup straight from the tap his sink filled with furry cups and plates baked-bean red. Didn't touch the beer no not for me but stayed up late with Kev. His red hound licking dregs out of cans big wet-black eyes and pointed face like party hat. Bitch sleeps on Kev's bed head on pillow stretched out on back with legs in air like dead spider

how to gut a fish

fucking weird I said

Not great at spooning he laughs shows me boot marks on her muzzle and old lumps of broken bone *had it rough this girl sure who am I to say sleep on the floor*

Kev says I can stay a while with him says I'm well shot of you Ellen well shot. I'm not a violent man no not a violent man but when he said that wanted to grab his skull and crush his eyeballs hear them pop. Can't though big heart on Kev good lad to take me in

room going spare anyway he says *my cousin Shona dead a year*

now space filled up with me although little pieces of Shona still there under bed. Hair bobbins purple tealights fingernail clippings. Poor girl awful sad young and all but Kev says born with a gloom in her and couldn't shake it. So better Shona sleeping in the ground and me sleeping in her bed. Sometimes dream of her. Taste canal water in my mouth but wake with the thirst. I feel her there in the dark the black fear comes on me again Ellen—

this road familiar now traffic lights walking man turned green maybe through here? but no wrong street wrong square don't know this place after all. This side of city tall houses eyes all around though curtains closed probably just cunts asleep beside other cunts. Newsagent's only place open now spilling light shutters cranking up. Little brown man with sweeping brush piles of newspapers tied up with plastic outside back door. Hi you looking at me hi? He's looking down again look up you think I'm scum not worth looking at but could buy a newspaper lean over shake my head tut-tut at front page laugh say what a head-line and pull out from pile and hand over €2

morning he says

no won't get the paper no fucking time for that yeah just like you suspected not buying paper. But I'll go into the shop anyway get water the thirst on me I will I won't why you looking at me? I will I don't and too late now. Looking back at shop now in you go little man scuttle under metal shutters and leave sweeping brush behind. I come back give brush a kick hah knocked it over hah now fallen against postcard tree. Little man watching me yeah watch me I'm gone. Did you see the way he looked at me Ellen—

maybe could go stay with Mam instead of Kev but her mouth full of wetness. Adult nappies and burnt electric blankets little chair with a hole in it for shit-ting. Two cats is it three? spending all her pension on drugs for a fucking cat that can't leave her bed

poor wee Tiger he needs me

poor nothing fucking Tiger should've been dead years ago all the Tigers of the world should be dead but for fucking mams and their pensions. She shites on to the cats at the neighbours at the walls like her mouth needs to stay open to let out pressure or head will swell up turn blue. Even talks to Dad still calls out to him from the kitchen

tea is it?

thirty years gone Dad is and priest said

peacefully at the end thank God

but what a liar he was. No peace in lostness no peace in yellow-filmed eyes foam at the lips tongue pressed down on teeth. How cold the room got then how cold and Mam on my shoulder heavy heavier than ever before. But my boy won't feel that cold won't see me yellow eyes not knowing won't feel the weight of you Ellen. Have a plan instead a good plan seen it on telly empty syringe fill it up with air. Find vein in arm and in it goes there it goes. Air bubble eases up and around to make gap enough to keep heart from squeezing burning shoving blood around and then mind will slip away and I'm gone. Cause I'm a Tiger too body rotting the pain in the mornings worst of all roll over in my bed cry with the pain of it knives in my kidneys. See my plan my boy how good I am to you do you see Ellen—

turn left then right here across road have to find green cross panic now my boy is coughing all alone. Pigeon hopping along in gutter watching me too. Head cocked walk like boxer feet melted into pink-black knuckles. Never see bird skeletons do you Ellen maybe rooftops lined with bones clogging up drains must be a little bird graveyard somewhere a little place to die. Or maybe birds never die never change immortal like jellyfish saw that documentary too

always learning things you say to me Ellen *always learning*

how to know though can't tell pigeons apart not like people no father's eyebrows or crooked noses or birthmarks. But this one has gnarly right foot tied up with string in purple knot yes will remember these feet remember this green-purple head because

the structural iridescence of pigeon plumage

use it to show off that's it. My head still pounding blood cold air clean breath stretch out over rooftops into sky. But cold suddenly heavy clouds pressing down on city on me. My fingers white at the end give them a flick-flick to warm but all blood stuck down by my guts churning in circles heat is rising there. Oh no it was only a sup from the tap but still the urge comes on fast and hard like fire. My bladder pushing up against belt oh the heat of it the burn. Here's an armpit of an alley no one around to see me quick unzip piss. Hot burning trickle just a trickle after all that fuck's sake wet cold drips. Will ask chemist after cough bottle in quiet voice for help

thirst getting worse and *pain in back*

and pink piss droplets on yesterday's boxers. Still wearing yesterday's boxers you wouldn't like that you'd think it's rank. Still carrying you behind my eyes Ellen you're always—

turn down this street. Here's a café bleeding out coffee morning smell such a nice mouthfeel. But makes you sick now Ellen you can't stand the smell. Showed me the scan you did I saw tiny bean swimming thumping swelling into little sister for our boy. Little bean when did she start growing? That time your curling yellow hair across the pillow your mouth open gripping my thighs and lifting you up against the wall Ellen your chafe on me and happy little bruise on your shoulder we laughed at it called it love. Was it that night or the other the half-sleeping one

go on if you want you said

and I said no

but it's a deal you said *love is a card game and bodies are chips*

so I went all right but only because I was bursting needed it but gently and you kissed me after. Hope it was that one the gentle sleeping one not the wall-fuck don't want new little kidney bean coming out already battered. Your brother did enough battering Ellen but he's gone now for good. Put a carpet knife against his ballsack when he spat on you in the pub after our boy's christening and held it there

if you touch her

if you call her

if you ever come back to see your godson

mantis

but he's gone off to England now or who the fuck cares. You cry sometimes but better out than in better off no brother than that brother Ellen I swear I—

finally relief there's a pharmacy green plus sign inside a plus sign inside another. Up steps fast knees through sliding glass doorbell ding

howiya morning

morning

eye-hurt brightness inside. Short round man behind counter with black squiggle hair above ears like cartoon and sweat armpit patches

need a cough bottle junior the pink one please

any allergies or other drugs sweaty man asks

no no

well yes just the steroids for his lungs tiny white tablets six at a time. Make him mental make him swing out of door handles chase neighbour's dog around the garden make him eat like four horses starved. But better that than the cough the tight chest scared white eyes. Nodding sweaty man goes to look for cough bottle. Keep shoulders in careful now pocket hands don't touch a thing. Wait. Wait breathe. Feels like back in Gran's house tiny china statues horses dogs saints I broke one once Padre Pio knocked his head right off sat it back on shoulders no problem. Gran went to her grave never knowing she's burning in hell for headless saint I'm sorry Gran. Remember to breathe. Walk aisles of plastic bottles pink purple green. Vitamins iron calcium zinc folic acid all of them healthy mum healthy baby. Exfoliating conditioning luxurious refreshing cosmetic you don't need a thing my Ellen—

sweaty man now picking boxes off shelves pill packets bright popping foil blisters. Why wet armpits so early in soft place this bright-light place music goes tinkle no need for sweat? Up on the crane at work above docks yes hell-sweat. First heat from the rise up to cabin the city dropping away then damp cold fear shirt peel away from back of chair. Starlings nesting on the crane jib this year eggs hatched and then chicks fell all the way down or flew maybe flew maybe caught the wind in their beaks and flew. Nearly all quiet up so high but wind runs through cab and cries oh it wails so supervisor says

just keep your eyes on the jib and we won't see the colour of your brain

to me stacking containers red to green then green to red above neon dots of men working twist locks and lashing them down. No jacks up there so have to hold it in or else fill plastic bottle up with yellow piss close it tight tuck it safe into jacket for climb down. City tiny from above in cabin like video game my boy loves to play. He builds towers factories schools roads then sends in a tornado tsunami earthquake burns his cities down then builds them up again. Feel I could reach out my

hands stretch my fingers touch boats coming over horizon. Chimneys first then cargo stacks then deck
that's how you know the world is round
or maybe another crane out there somewhere in
the ocean layering up ships block by block by block.
When crane swoops my belly left behind and head
fuzzes up then sweat pure ice and the wind sings yes
I remember Ellen I'm careful up there—

another bint comes out behind counter young
woman orange face thick across belly but no tits
yawning talking to other small man such a shower of
talk. She says
messy one last night
how late was it where did Dan go off to
almost forgot his brother's wedding next week
don't give a shit about Dan let him choke let him
die let his brother's cock rot off. Sweaty man closes all
cupboards checks under desk looks up at me finally
pink one was it? Sorry no don't have that one
sweaty man says *sorry* hands me a big fat *sorry*
instead of pink cough bottle. I'll wrap it up put a bow
on it have a white plastic spoon of *sorry* my lad suck
it down now don't mind the taste you can have biccy
afterwards as long as you finish your *sorry*. Orange
woman staring now eyes falling out of piggy face no
more chat about Dan's brother why'd you stop? Look
down my fist is slammed in among the packets of
green throat sweets my knuckles throbbing now. Try

swallow my scream but sticks like morning pills in throat my eyes glued to small man's face

please I say *please*

but lips won't open just trapped moan in my mouth feels like drowning here in this dry place. Sweaty man stepping away hands up

no trouble now Sarah would you call the Guards

and I stagger away shampoo bottles skitter across floor. Out the door leave shocked faces bell ringing behind me I tried Ellen—

back down the street again. Panic now a clothes-line wrapped around my chest it hurts the tightness. Here's my shoes lifting one and the other just take one step and lift but heavy swollen feet the pain the pain of pulling whole body I am dying thing attached to cement. Take a knife cut a slit drain out the pus the rot. Might bleed me empty but then wrap me up and no more rubbing no more hurt. Back to armpit alley-way ground sit against cold wall bladder full of heat again. Pigeon claw-scatter but different bird to earlier two full feet healthy ones I remember I remember. Swallow my spit. Breathe breathe. But still fishing hook in my heart. Wrinkled wood-pit inside soft pink-yellow peach fuzz I bite down break my teeth. No medicine for our boy Ellen I couldn't—

time to rewind it play scene again. You're dozing on my lap your warm cheeks twitching eyes and deep-voiced man on telly explains

mantis

the mantis shrimp's unique evolutionary adaptation
want to wake you to watch this. Bony thick shell
stomatopod predators store energy in a specialised region
of the carapace
that was the word carapace all jointed down to the
bum with shy tail curled under. Mantis shrimp hides
in rocks bubbles of air pushing out then fish wanders
by and whip-crack claw comes out to club on head.
Replay now rewind slow it down
special jack-knifing mechanism to stun prey
see-through head feelers poking out hinge arm all
folded up. Ready now here comes a fish swimming
by wait for it wait for it bang!
fast as a speeding bullet
So warm in my lap you are wake up and see Ellen—
and then later on hot anger in your face and eyes
sagging. Spit on lips hands on belly you tell me
no good for him no good for her
not our boy any more just your boy not our new
baby just yours. Then my fist curled back all by itself
folded up wrist-elbow-shoulder like a hinge and then
came the flick whip-crack thud. Not a violent man
no but my mantis arm just it just and the force spun
you around it just did it on its own. Your mouth an
O a great O of surprise but nothing came out and
slow-motion fall your hair spilled out on the ground
around curve of your stomach you shouldn't have
made me Ellen—

how to gut a fish

now no cough bottle for my boy his dry tight wheeze. Your eyes Ellen will know no good no good for him no good for baby girl. Overhead sun sliding away out of alleyway already. Not noon yet but dark now daylight used up shifted to other streets other places better things to light up today than this broken pile of bones where is pigeon graveyard let me go there I am ready

peacefully at the end thank God

my bladder swell again against tight jeans the pain no peace here. Just let it go and piss comes squeaking out the burn. Warm wet-spread the relief ten seconds of warmth worth hours of cold but I'm sinking into grit-floor shards of glass small grey stones slip into boots and my fingers shake. Ellen my hands I can't see—

your fingers pressed to floor kneeling you
steady against the kitchen floor but too late I am
so sorry Ellen I didn't mean—

hold fast

The black, five-sided pillars tower over the sand like the pipes of a church organ. The strange angles are familiar to Cath from school trips to the Giant's Causeway, and a thousand postcards from her childhood. But the rocks off the coast of Antrim are a warm brown; moss grows freely between the cracks and tourists have worn the sharp edges down with their footfall and the shutters of their cameras. These gun-metal columns are severe and wild; they could have sprung up yesterday rather than thousands of years ago. Waves crash into caves all along the shoreline and an audience of seabirds is frozen against the wind.

The café perched above the beach is under construction, says a sign, spelled out in small Icelandic lettering and in larger English words. Cath imagines that this work must be constant, that the kneading of the North Atlantic against the coastline requires constant buttressing and repairs. A workman takes his tea in the café's back room, telling a story to the girl behind the counter. They laugh together, great intense huffs, like a shot of the Icelanders' fiery *brennivín*; a joke that doesn't lighten the air around them but stays private and close to their mouths.

Cath had rolled her eyes at the girl in commiseration when the American woman in the queue in front of her had tried to pay in dollars, but she hadn't noticed, even when Cath let out a carefully pronounced *takk*, following it with a *fyrir* for emphasis. There are tourists and *tourists*, she has learned, and being from Northern Ireland, even living in Scotland, is less of an offence than most; the locals treat her as a long-lost cousin rather than a rude, inexplicable stranger.

A monstrous tour bus pulls into the car park, silent behind the weatherproof glass window of the café. Tourists spill out and regroup on the stones. A muddle of middle-aged German women and a handful of college students; American, or Canadian at the least. After only a few days in Iceland, Cath has become good at cataloguing *tourists* by the placement of a camera, the layering of their waterproofs, whether their eyes fall upwards or downwards at the first sight of a waterfall, a sheet of volcanic rock, a blackened plain.

She sips her hot chocolate as they pick their way down, ignoring the clamour of warning signs that are the only colour against the grey of the beach. Blue for dangerous waves, red for rockfalls; a yellow triangle shows the outline of a swimmer with a bar across his face. *Never turn your back on the ocean*, spelled out in a dozen languages.

That morning, the hostel manager had run his eye over her itinerary at the breakfast table and had tapped the beach with his finger. *Here there are sneaky waves*, he said, solemnly. *We call them Chinese takeaways.* Cath had laughed, awkwardly, but the man had been surprised by her laughter.

She raises her cup to her lips in time with the workman, trying to match his thirst, but her hot chocolate runs out before he finishes his tea. The sun is sinking behind the hills already. Time to move on. The GPS on her phone is sluggish; she scrolls through a few reviews of the area while she waits to update her location.

★★★ *Reynisfjara Beach* – *amazing basalt columns but too many tourists climbing them trying to get a picture. Scenes from* Game of Thrones *were shot here. Decent café. Freaky waves, be careful!!!* ★★★

In Glasgow, Senan is woken by the cat clawing at a corner of the bedsheet that hangs down over the edge of the mattress. He rolls over immediately and refreshes the aurora forecast on his phone. It is centred on Reykjavik, although he knows Cath must have moved east by now. A ring of green light squats over the Arctic Circle. The forecast is hovering around three, which means possible aurora sightings, but visibility is poor due to heavy cloud cover.

He knows the seven-day itinerary off by heart. Cath had planned their route around the island without him paying much attention, but once she had left, alone, he had memorised it, breaking the days into bite-sized chunks. The beginning and end of the trip are marked on his kitchen calendar; he is lingering in the crossed-out section in between.

Senan tries to rebury himself in a mound of blankets, but the cat jumps on his bed and begins kneading at his hair.

———

The driving is easier than Cath had expected. Although the ring road around the island is narrow, the air is so flat and clear the approach of a car can be seen from ten minutes away; twin pinpricks of light blinking over the hills and dips of the coastal route, growing larger with each disappearance and reappearance.

Senan had booked the rental car online, upgrading their package to a 4×4 jeep with full coverage without asking her opinion. He had been convinced that the rental company had a good scam going; the standard package came without chip insurance, and most of the roads outside of Reykjavik are gritted during the winter months. *A single pebble in the windscreen, and bam, they've got you on the hook for thousands*, he had said. A single slip of the wheels on black ice and you're gone.

At noon, Cath reaches a wood-and-slate building encasing a lava exhibition. In the foyer, a relief map of the island shows recent volcanic activity, and screens replay historic eruptions. She feels her rage pulsing in time with the throb of the magma, roaring to life out of underwater craters. She pulls off her gloves and her warming skin mottles under orange and red stage lights. The floor rumbles, clearing its throat under her feet, and the anger subsides again.

She reaches the next remote hotel at four o'clock, but it is already dark. There is nothing to do, so she eats her dinner of thick fish soup early, out of boredom. On her way back from the restaurant to the hotel, she dawdles, looking for the Northern Lights, but a light flurry of sleet is congesting the sky.

In her double room, the bedsheets are rough and camel-coloured, and the water from the tap smells like sulphur. A couple are fucking in the next room; also out of boredom, she assumes.

★★★★★ *Lava Centre* – *Kids loved it! Giant screens, rumbling floors, lots of fun. Toilets the best on the coast! But high admission – could skip and check Wiki page for volcanoes;)* ★★★★★

how to gut a fish

The craft market opens at eleven but Senan is there by half past ten. He wasn't supposed to display today, so he wants to make sure his spot isn't claimed by another vendor. The stalls fill up quickly, and the clove-hung smell of mulled wine begins to make his mouth water.

He takes his time laying out his jewellery pieces on a black silk sheet. He has experimented with grouping by type, by stone and by price, but each day he decides on a different arrangement. Today, he lays out fine, threaded earrings alongside thick silver bangles; glass stone rings at child's-eye level, and whisper-thin chains dangling from overhead spokes. Some pieces complement each other, like coloured flowers in a vase, and others he feels need to be separated, like bickering children.

Maria is selling dried seaweed from East Neuk of Fife in the stall beside him, but she keeps her eyes to her work, cutting and sorting. Her apron is green today, her hair wild and the colour of storm-washed sand. She hasn't asked why he has appeared at the market this morning after all, why he isn't a thousand kilometres away, why he isn't with Cath in an over-priced hotel, why they aren't arguing over the satnav, daring each other to taste fermented shark.

Senan pedals the polishing machine once or twice to warm it up, and lays out his embossed business cards. He feels Maria's mouth open behind him, senses her trying and failing to say something.

hold fast

The flight from Glasgow to Reykjavik had been cheap, surprisingly so, although the cost of the accommodation made up for it. Just before take-off, the flight attendant had come along with a tablet and had marked the seat beside Cath as absent. She had considered telling them in advance at the check-in counter, but when they called Senan's name over the airport intercom, in increasingly brisk tones, their shared annoyance had salved something in her.

She had downloaded a travel safety app in the airport's waiting area, in case of an accident in a remote part of the island. Two large rectangular buttons take up almost the entire screen of her phone, marked CHECK IN and EMERGENCY, one in green and the other in red. On the road, she opens it every hour to send an update soaring across the island to a central tower, the GPS twanging to her location like an elastic band. She feels guilty of annoying someone every time she presses the green button.

Afternoon, and the sunset sky is stained with streaks of low cloud. The jeep edges forward between two lines of white, her ankle straining, playing the brakes like a bellows. The B&B is another twenty-three kilometres away. She does some calculations: an hour at this creeping, nervous speed, or she could pick it up and go faster, trust in the rubbered metal of engineering, the grip of the tyres holding fast to the gritted road. A sign swims out of the darkness, reminding her to ARRIVE ALIVE. Another asks *ERU BELTIN SPENNT?* above two hands belting together around a waist.

Full dark, and a softening of night appears in the sky behind her. It takes some time for Cath to be certain of the patch of brightness in the sky, falling in and out of focus as she takes quick glimpses upwards at the rear-view mirror. She pulls over and turns off the headlamps to let her eyes adjust, her heart pounding. She has heard that the aurora in real life doesn't look anything like photographs, and it can take up to ten minutes for the human eye to adapt to darkness. She closes her eyes to speed up the process. When she opens them, a point of light is piercing the clouds, but it is soft and creamy, like coffee-foam. She checks the guidebook tossed on the back seat, types a few trembling words into the search engine on her phone. Her eyes find the reviews and the beginnings of a wild and primal awe drain away.

She doesn't realise she is crying until the brine reaches her lips.

★★ *Imagine Peace Tower – this is an outdoor 'artwork', a tower of light by Yoko Ono in memory of John Lennon. What a bloody nuisance this light pollution is, it ruined our search for the Northern Lights* ★★

hold fast

After the market, Senan takes the motorway exit for Cath's house automatically, and by the time he realises what he has done it is too late to merge back, so he drives ten kilometres in the wrong direction before he can find a turning point.

At the sound of his key in the lock, the cat startles from the couch and slinks over to the tiny window. He lets it out on to the fire escape, even though a light rain has begun to fall. The soft pads of its mottled paws press against the mesh of the wire flooring and it trots, legs high, as if stepping on hot sand.

Senan checks his leftover stock again, counting. He sold twenty-one pieces of jewellery at the market today, a good day, especially for January. Maria had lifted her hand in a half-wave when she left; the bile of shame had risen in his throat as he ignored her.

He fingers a thick, curved bracelet, gently stretching it, and sees it clasped against Cath's freckled skin. He wants to shape her under a blue-hot torch like a piece of silver, move her over the heat until her spine bends. She'll call him tonight. She won't. She will. She should but she won't.

He sits by the window as he eats his dinner, watching for a shepherd's sky. A red haze from the west will mean that her day has been fine, that dark, swollen clouds haven't burst on top of her and sent her spiralling into a ditch.

how to gut a fish

Later, he checks the news for accidents, for heavy jeeps falling in slow motion over spindly bridges; wheels grit-spinning against frozen streams; flushes of meltwater; thick flows of lava pouring down exposed slopes. A headline catches under his fingers – *Tourist Drowns at Reynisfjara Beach*. The heat of terror continues its upward rush to his face even after he sees the article is dated six months ago.

Cath pulls off the road once she catches the smell of sulphur and checks the guidebook again. Other tourists accompany her up the path from the car park, picking their way carefully around violet, spitting pools of geothermal water. The hellish smell is unbearable; she wraps her scarf over her mouth and the wool squeaks against her teeth. The water is as blue as a baby's eye.

A few kilometres later, she pulls in at another sign and gets out of the car. There is a deep, dry gouge in the earth, running across the land from the mountains to the sea, splitting the vast lava fields in two. At first, she is puzzled by its presence in this wet, cold place. The fissure reminds her of an old riverbed in the fields outside her parents' house in Derry; in hot summers it would dry out almost completely and she and her brother would look for fishbones in the cracked soil. She had once found a dinosaur tooth, a long, smooth shaft that was shaped vaguely like a triangle. She took it into school the next day; the teacher pressed it firmly between his thumb and fingers, and it fell into pieces of compacted dirt.

She reads the information board and realises that the gully is the dividing line between tectonic plates, separating two continents. WELCOME TO AMERICA, a sign on one side says, WELCOME TO EUROPE the other. The iron bridge over the gap crackles under her feet as she tries to see down into the belly of the earth, but the fissure is only as deep as she is tall. She walks over to the American side and closes her eyes, imagines she feels the earth moving, the continents pulling apart.

In the thermal baths, an Englishman with shoulders full of tattoos tells her about his daughter back home; how she had been born with the skin of a butterfly. The floor of the pool is lined with the silt of other people's bodies. They wade chest-high laps around the baths, talking softly until the sun goes down and they are the only two left in the water. At the side closest to the hot springs, where the water almost scalds, the Englishman strokes the soft part of his fist against the taut cloth over Cath's breasts and eases his index and middle finger between her legs.

Afterwards, she floats on a purple pool noodle and looks again for the Northern Lights, but the clouds are still low and thick. The air is bitter, burning ice.

how to gut a fish

★ *Gamla Laugin (Secret Lagoon) – The day after I swam in the thermal baths I got skin blisters and other nasty stuff. Yuck! My boyfriend's hiking boots were stolen – wound up going home in flip-flops* ★

It's illegal to pick living seaweed from underwater forests, Maria had told him, when they went for a festive drink after the New Year's Day market. But clumps that have been washed above the tideline during a storm, or grow out of rockpools – those are fair game.

She had explained the picking and drying process over sushi and rice wine. Senan had followed the curve of her fingers as she traced out the shapes of the different types of seaweed with a chopstick: egg wrack, kelp, mermaid's tresses and dabberlocks.

You use a knife to cut a piece from the fronds, she said, demonstrating with a floret of broccoli, *but leave the root, the holdfast, anchored to the rock, and the stem will regrow.*

Like taking rose cuttings from a garden, he had said, and her orange-painted mouth turned up at the corners, delighted that he had understood.

When Maria touched his arm so gently, in her apartment after dinner, her bared skin had been warm, and her body even warmer. Senan rolls over in bed with the shame of the memory.

Wherever they go, Cath is always cold. Taking the chill from her body – opening his jacket to enclose her, rubbing her feet, clasping her hands between his – had been a point of pride to him. *Cold hands mean a warm heart*, she says.

When he sat down to confess what he had done, she had started to shiver before he even began. Warm hands, cold heart.

———

Night-driving again, and Cath stops to pee at the side of the road. The headlights fall on moss, grey in the monochrome night, but she knows in daylight they melt purple, blue and green over the volcanic rock. A white sign says that injury to the moss takes seventy years to heal. As she squats, she counts to distract herself from the cold. Seventy years. Twice her lifetime. Three years of fortnights. Fourteen batches of fingers. Ten broken mirrors.

There is a huffing, uneven shuffle behind her and her stomach drops hard and into the ground. She pulls her trousers back over her hips and dives towards the open car door to grab a torch, eyes burning. She points it into the darkness.

Only the lower half of the small, fat horse is visible in the yellow dusting of light, its chestnut flanks ice-sprinkled and heaving. There is no protective fence on the road here, nothing to keep her contained, and she steps into the ditch towards it, pockmarked earth shifting under her boots. The red-brown horse shudders under her touch and leaps away, snorting in surprise.

Suddenly the cold rams its way down her throat and her lungs contract with the sting of it. Her left boot catches in a frozen puddle and she goes down, bare hands scraping against the burning grass. She crawls back to the jeep on her hands and knees, a cold and breathless fear in her heart.

★★★ *Route 1 (Ring Road)* – *Pitch-dark, narrow road and incredibly strong crosswinds. Driving this route at night is not for the faint-hearted. Kids said it was like flying through space!* ★★★

It has begun to rain in Glasgow, and the light has turned orange and strange. Senan cannot tell what time of the day it is. Above him, his neighbour is practising on his saxophone. The cat scratches at the window, and Senan stares at it for a long minute before letting it in.

Cath prefers dogs to cats; she thinks love should be unconditional.

———

Another day of driving and stopping and seeing and driving and stopping. It is almost dark when Cath reaches the glacier, and she is on a narrow bridge over the lagoon before she even realises. The rumble strips hum under the jeep's thick wheels. She turns off the road and down to the ocean, although the calving glacier is to her left, and the warm red glow of a gift shop sings in the air.

Out from the beach, a punctured shepherd's night has set a drop of crimson in the sea, and a fertile smoke sits low on the water. Ridge-shaped waves creep towards land, carrying white shocks of ice filled with the dark ash of eruptions. On the sand, prongs of diamonds shine on the beach, and a copse of camera tripods has sprung up to capture the sunset refracting through the glassy ice.

An elderly couple try to include her in the warmth of their shared awe, but Cath ignores them. She walks along the beach until they disappear into the twilight. She tries to convince herself that she sees ribbons of astral light undulating above the beach, but the sky is as dry and bare as brittle bones.

★★★★ *Diamond Beach – Could only find small pieces of ice but still lovely. Getting white balance right in photographs can be tricky. The sand is v. black and the ice is v. white* ★★★★

Her last night and it has begun to rain, camouflaging the sky one final time. There is nothing to do but sit in the hotel bar, drink expensive beer and talk to the other travellers.

Why did you decide to come to Iceland? she is asked, again and again. Each lie she tells circles closer to the truth.

Because she is on an adventure to find herself after the death of her spouse.

Because she has voted for Iceland in the Eurovision for ten years straight.

Because she is a writer, researching folklore for her next book.

Because she wanted to stitch her heart back together.

Because she felt the iron pull of the aurora; needed to bare herself under the green–blue lights.

———

At the airport check-in desk, there is a queue, even though it is so early in the morning as to be still yesterday. Two white and worried faces float over the counter. An announcement comes down from the ceiling: the flight is delayed. Cath shifts in her seat but is unwilling to give it up. A young mother trots her baby up and down in her lap as she watches the large screen. An hour later, the flight is delayed again.

When the flight number disappears from the departures board entirely, a staff member is sent around to give them conciliatory vouchers for the single restaurant in the airport. Voices begin to spiral from private to public and a well-dressed man attempts to force himself down the darkened corridor to the plane; two blond security men arrive and restrain him against the wall. The intercom pings to life but it is a reminder not to leave baggage unattended for any reason.

The smell of the fish jerky in Cath's handbag, a gift for the cat, begins to leak out, although it is sealed tightly in plastic. She had stared at the packaging for twenty minutes in the duty-free shop, walking circles around bottles of liquor and fridge magnets, coming back to it again and again. A woman had pressed gently on her arm to ask if she needed help; Cath shook her head and hurried the jerky over to the sales counter.

Behind the check-in desk, a flight attendant rips her finely pinned cap from her head and tosses it to the floor. The baby begins to wail.

★ *Keflavík Airport – Dreadful way to end a lovely trip. Unfriendly staff and no information signs. Waiting area has no electricity plugs. Entire country was broke and is being kept alive by tourists – wouldn't hurt to smile!* ★

Senan sits in the short-term car park at Glasgow Airport, refreshing the arrivals screen on his phone again and again. The roads were clear, this early in the morning, and he had pulled into the airport sooner than he had intended, sand-eyed in the warmth coming from the car's heater.

He had dozed off, for what felt like a year, waking in a panic – he had missed Cath's flight, missed his chance to see the fumbling emotion in her face as she walked through the barriers and saw him, missed the point where he could insert a crowbar into their relationship and heave – but only a few minutes had passed. That had been two hours ago, but he is afraid to sleep again, so the radio is blasting loudly and the driver-side window is cracked open.

He checks his phone again, searches the name of the airline. A muttering is beginning online; a trickle at first and then a stream, until questions and demands are being hammered out into the ether with the regularity of machine-gun fire. He sees posts from London, Dallas, Iowa; entire rows of exclamation marks and faces appear. Breaking news and headlines begin to litter his news feed: *Budget Airline Bankrupt, Passengers Left Stranded*. The word stranded appears again and again, like a bloom of seaweed on a beach.

Senan gets slowly out of his car and stretches, slapping his legs to bring them back to life. He goes towards the terminal, to find a kiosk selling coffee; somebody, anybody to talk to.

He will call her. He will. He won't. He should but he won't.

hold fast

It is still dark, even above the harsh lights of the airport, but daylight is beginning to skitter into the world. Across the sky, red streaks of light bleed into the steam from the terminal, turning them into boiling flows of molten rock.

instinct

i

When the dog first arrived, we were pleased. The seller dropped it off in an old red van with no licence plate, dust reaching up as far as the door handles and a wire mesh behind the driver's seat. When the rear doors opened, we saw a tail thumping dully against the carpeted floor and a flat, tawny skull weaving over and back between two gaunt shoulder blades.

The notice had popped up online in a neighbourhood swap group. DOG, FREE TO A GOOD HOME, and a picture of a long-nosed mutt with black, button eyes. We had previously agreed not to get a pet – we lived in an apartment, our working hours were wrong, it was never the right time – and had resigned ourselves to smiling at dogs in the street.

Then the baby came, and our days were taken up with wet things. The spare room stopped being spare, and white noise and the sound of waves crashing over distant rocks found a place in our dreams. For a year and change, the corners of our lives softened around the sweet core of him, and we laughed at the people we had been. But eventually, the baby picked himself up off the floor, our jobs settled back to routine, and we found brief periods of time where our hands weren't full and hung strangely by our sides.

In the end, getting the dog was an impulsive thing, a matter of our eyes meeting over the baby's head, three clicks and an exchange of phone numbers while we sat in front of a movie on a Sunday night. We felt pleased with ourselves, like we were ticking some piece of unurgent housework off the list early.

FREE TO A GOOD HOME, the advert said, but when the van arrived, we had a €50 note ready anyway; we had no car so the delivery was appreciated. The man refused the money with a shake of his head. We assumed that we were a good home. There didn't seem to be a test to pass.

The dog had no collar, so we shepherded it upstairs to our apartment quickly before our neighbours could see. Animals weren't allowed in our lease, but after years of neglected maintenance and rent hikes, we felt entitled to break a few clauses in the opposite direction. Besides, we were sure that our downstairs neighbours had a python; we had once seen the flaking fishnet of a skin-shed in the compost bin.

The driver didn't say goodbye to the dog before getting back into the van, which didn't strike us as strange at the time. Later, we would remember the uneven curve of the man's back, the coarse wool of his jumper, but not the shape of his face.

ii

The dog was knobbly thin and had dew claws like marlin spikes, and oily tear tracks spilling from dark, viscous eyes. Its short fur was tawny brown, with a suggestion of stripes rippling against its ribs. It smelled of nothing except warm dust and antiseptic, but to be sure, we put it in the shower to wash it because we didn't have a bathtub. It glared at us, wagging its tail uncertainly, as we herded it with towels, its long legs skittering against the slippery porcelain. By the end, we were as wet as flowers after rain and our laughs came out high-pitched and feverish. The baby shrieked at us in approval from his perch on the bed and clapped at the spectacle.

Afterwards, the dog tasted the air around the soft, oval basket we had spent too much money on and curled up on the hardwood floor beside it instead. It pressed its nose into its thigh to watch us move around the room, and it sighed often, the very expression of resignation.

That evening, we found out that the dog was infested with parasites. The wriggling white lines in its droppings were hypnotic; little streaks of life exposed to light for the first time, struggling towards the sky. After we dosed it, the threadworms came out in clumped knots, as the dog strained, wide-eyed, but at least they no longer wiggled and waved.

A few days later, we had to deworm ourselves too, because although the dog wasn't overly interested in licking us, the baby would let it clean his hands after each meal. He proudly announced at crèche that he had worms in his tummy; this coming on top of an incident with head lice resulted in an after-school meeting with a childcare worker, and the eventual shaving of the baby's head. The fine bones of his skull shone blue and white under the apartment's bay windows as he sulked.

Even so, the baby liked the dog. He wasn't a grabby child, but he was impulsive, so we spoke to him sternly about the evils of pinching and tail-pulling. He hadn't found a frequent use yet for his tongue, preferring to keep it pressed between his clean, white teeth, but he nodded like a diplomat and filed it all away. His approaches were wide, toddling circles, spiralling inwards, while the dog rotated in the opposite direction, trying to keep the baby in its line of sight; having a strain of hound in it, its eyes were hare-like on the side of its skull, split by a broad snout and a dry, cracking nose. When they met in the middle, the dog would allow the baby a clumsy stroke or two on its flank, then slip away, flitting from under the table, to the bed, to a nook behind the front door.

But after a time, trust began to creep in. The baby would sit on the floor and watch old cartoons, and the dog would slowly inch closer, until they were shoulder to shoulder, staring at the screen. Together, they watched bright creatures with bulging eyes and sing-song voices chasing each other in circles, until stopped short by the force of a frying pan, a brick wall, a neat package of red TNT. Then the baby would roar in delight at the screen, and the dog would startle away from him again.

The dog was resistant to learning commands, leading us to declare on alternate days that it was too stupid or too smart to obey us. It had been starved before it came to us, we were sure, because food was its only concern. Some instinct in the dog's mind had been broken, or encouraged, or withered away, because every second of every day was an attempt not to be hungry, to fill up an aching gap. At mealtimes, it emptied its own bowl in seconds, and its eyes followed our plates like an uncanny portrait. Overfeeding it did no good, as its stomach was likely to burst from the unfamiliar strain, although we did, bashfully, let it lick the fat from the frying pan after Sunday breakfasts. Butter was its favourite, real farm-house butter, although it would take yellow margarine at a pinch. Left sitting on the counter for more than a second or two and the butter would vanish. If we caught the thief quickly enough, we could scoop off the tongue-furrowed layer and salvage it, but if it went unnoticed there would only be an empty plastic container left, and the dog would produce squirting puddles of undigested fat out of both ends for days.

But mainly, it curved neatly around our lives like a snake sleeping on a branch. We came and went from home to crèche to work to crèche to home in a lazy pendulum, the dog startling to life every time a key sounded in the door. It always seemed vaguely surprised to see us again, as if we were a bizarre but pleasant dream recurring each day.

Our neighbours stopped us in the hall to compliment its improving health and rounding belly. We told them that it was perfect for life in the city and took it to sit outside expensive cafés with us.

The baby grew a little taller, and we kissed him and marked his height against the wall with a thick carpenter's pencil. Our house plants flourished. We put festive antlers on the dog at Christmas; it rubbed them off against a wire fence.

iii

When we all lost our jobs, the dog was uneasy. During the day, in the time that had been its alone, we now appeared, dressed in pyjamas and clutching the pieces of paper that came in the post. We had always wondered what it did while we were at work, but whatever it did became undone. Instead, it watched us nervously from under the table as we walked around the apartment, occasionally feeling at the walls and doorways to make sure they were still there.

instinct

We tried to keep ourselves busy; told ourselves that countless others were in the same boat, took a positive attitude to this unfamiliar stretching of time. We attended meetings at the welfare office, took evening course after course, trying to master esoteric skills that we would never apply. We tried crocheting in the mornings and coding in the evenings; weekends were indistinct lumps of excess time. We tore at the skin around our fingers while we queued for hours outside the post office, arguing the finer points of filled-out forms and pretending not to recognise our neighbours.

We still walked the dog in the mornings, after dropping the baby off at crèche, nodding at others and smiling at the sky. Sometimes other people would nod at us first, and we would have to smile back; it became a competition, an escalating race of wordless pleasantries, until our heads were stretched like meerkats. But eventually, the long loops around the river became routine to the dog as much as us – head down, legs whirring, it would still stop to nose at the weeds, but without much real interest. It was the walk of a worrier: we began to take each corner at a close angle to reach home again as fast as possible.

For the rest of the day, the dog would sit on the back of the armchair like a sentry and watch the street below, front paws extended to press against the glass, as if reassuring itself that in here was here and out there was there.

how to gut a fish

We sat instead on the couch in front of the tele-vision, watching an endless reel of red statistics; politicians and spokespeople with downcast faces, shoulders hunched and heads low; a shuffling of anxious crows offering apologies in one hand and a scolding in the other. The chorus of their state-ments began to bore us; we made a theatre stage of the living room and took turns delivering their lines. Sometimes we joined the dog; made viewing perches with our palms, sat our eyes in the crook between thumb and index finger, until it was time to collect the baby again and remember how to smile.

Outside, in the city, people stepped through their lives, in and out of doorways and offices and shaded alcoves, always in a hurry to get somewhere. The air became heavy and stale, carrying the ballast of other people's sighs. The shops whipped off and changed their signs like burlesque dancers. Traffic lights grew bags over their eyes, and cranes fell from cloud-streaked skies.

Colours and parades lined the streets below us, aimed at keeping the city's spirits up in these trying times: marching bands; groups of butterfly women rotating in saris; looming, eight-legged giants made of papier mâché taking shuddering steps, one limb at a time. Tourists came by to take photos of the fast-flowing river.

instinct

Our neighbours stopped talking to us in the hall-ways and the building filled up with silence. We moved in a rhythm with them, a one-two step, spinning up and down the corridors and stairs, flattening our bodies against walls to let each other pass by. The landings grew thick with a yellowing mulch of envelopes. We found arguments over bicycles and stereos where there had been only shrugs before.

The baby brought home pencil scratchings instead of smudged paint; his notebooks grew lines and grids spiderwebbed over the blank space. He began to wet the bed again, refusing to drink in fear of night-time accidents; instead we fed him chunky soup and juice frozen into ice-pops. We kissed him goodnight and in the morning he told us that he dreamed of running across deserts and dry places.

Eventually, we stopped going to meetings and courses; ran out of reasons to open the door. The baby stayed at crèche, for a time, until he didn't, and he spent all day building towers and crashing them down again on an old yoga mat in the kitchen. He caught fewer colds, then, away from the constant wash of other children, but his coughs, when they came, were deep, barking things and the dog would prick its ears up until they died away.

The dog began to follow us more closely, curling up on our feet if we sat and waiting outside the bathroom door while we rinsed ourselves in lukewarm water. In bed, we grabbed at each other so hard we left bruises. The dog cried and scraped at the bedroom door, running loops around the baby in the next room, once tumbling him off the couch in panic and on to the hardwood floor. The air in the apartment had the sharp rankness of an abandoned swimming pool.

iv

The television was the first to be cut off. Not that we minded, because we were committed to our street-watching at that stage, to lining up to press our faces against the damp glass, resting our elbows in smears of black mould for hours at a time. The baby joined us, turning away from his beloved cartoons with a sad smile. The dog seemed to miss them more than the baby; it took to stealing empty packets from the bin to shred in its basket.

The gas was next, which, in winter, was more of a problem, but we cut holes in our duvets and wore them like royal mantles, swinging our trains around in swirling pools of fabric. The first time we wore them, the baby laughed at us, and himself, and then he seemed to quieten again.

The electricity was the last to go, and it happened in the morning, which was good as it gave us daylight to put our things in order. Although, in truth, there wasn't much to do – the apartment had become barer each

instinct

day as our furniture faded away and what little dirt there was had been kept firmly outside the front door.

As evening crept in, we lit the last of our candles, drank from the tap until water dripped from our chins, and watered the houseplants one final time. The baby arranged his tower blocks in a straight, even line, and the yoga mat was rolled up, the dog whining gentle encouragement all the while.

In the centre of the darkened apartment, we lay down together on the wooden floor, the baby – although he had really, truly become a boy – in between us, his sweet, soft skull in the crook of our armpits. Carefully, oh so carefully, the dog stretched out its jaw and took us into its mouth; bare feet first, and then its lips covered our shins (unshaven, the last razor having rusted away). It swallowed for the first time at our knees, and then things went smoother: we slipped in like a minecart on rails, our pelvises causing the dog no problems at all. The dog's black and pink gums were flush with health, we were pleased to notice, before it swallowed again, and down we went, arms swaying bonelessly like the last pieces of spaghetti in a ceramic bowl.

star jelly

The full, hollow ribcage is laid out on the path under the February sun, rust-brown with points of white bone that jut from the smears of flesh. The long skull is still in place, sitting on vertebrae that curl around into a question mark and finish at a wide pelvis. Two uneven rows of flat-topped teeth make a jagged line of the jawbone; the missing incisors are dark rivets in an off-white horseshoe.

The four hikers sniff at the air for any foulness as they hang back, but the deer carcass has aged out of pungency. One takes a white staff of birch from the side of the path and hooks it under the ribcage, raising it above his head as a totem, chanting like a villain from an old Technicolor cartoon. The others groan at his crudeness and flap their hands to make him stop. He swings the torso around in a circle, letting it fly off across the ditch and into the thick Sitka forest, where it clatters against a raft of branches before disappearing into the dark.

It is early on a Sunday, around half past eleven, and the memory of rain slicks the hikers' windcheaters to their skin. Pavel takes the lead as they press onwards and upwards away from the car park, moving from the tarmacked track on to the stone slabs of the forest trail. He jumps over the ankle-twisting crevices in the path, pushing uphill too fast for the others to keep up. He is pretending to be brighter and fitter than he is, mainly because he doesn't want to see the annoyance in his cousin's face. Pavel feels bad about convincing him to drive them all the way out here to the soft slopes of the Wicklow Mountains, with what looks like a throbbing hangover at that. He hopes that this energy will lift Ultan's mood to match his own, like a barge rising in a canal lock.

Ultan had been red-eyed when he picked them up, and his auburn hair was lank before they even got out of the car, but not from a hangover. He is a weed smoker rather than a drinker, after what it had done to his head in college, but he had been up late with a housemate who was determined to finish a bottle of supermarket vodka on his own. His friend had only run out of tears at around four in the morning, but Ultan had stayed awake in the white noise of a comfortable armchair and hadn't even needed to open his eyes when his phone buzzed with his cousin's early message. A small finger of hope had driven him out and into the car: the possibility of a sugar-spun bridge of words with Lauren – Pavel's ex-girlfriend, if you could call her that; if a drunken fuck and a simultaneous depressive episode in their second year of college constituted a relationship – because Ultan senses that they are both the type to read the book before the film comes out. He shortens his stride in the hopes that Lauren will catch up to him and they can begin a gentle argument.

But Lauren is dull and distracted today, except for at the very beginning, when she had launched herself out of the car and up the steps cut into the hill, taking them in twos, shouting *hup-hup-hup* while a tin water bottle jangled against her hip. She has come straight off the night shift in the hostel and has another shift tonight; she hopes that the hike will tire her out enough for a long afternoon sleep. But the adrenaline of exhaustion has begun to leak away, and she takes the white staff of birch out of Pavel's hands to lean on as she walks. Her hair is swept back by a strip of patterned fabric, but chestnut curls still float around her forehead.

A few metres behind her, Elena's eyes also water with tiredness; she has travelled so much this month that red spots of chafe have appeared between her thighs. The rash is wet and fiery and she falls further behind the others to pull the fabric around her groin away from her skin for stinging moments of relief. She is a long-term guest at the hostel Lauren works at, and has come along for the hike, although she was only half-invited, and half a friend at that. But Elena's visa has run out and she is trying to drink the entire country in; racing from cliffsides to trad sessions to exhibitions. It's not that she has nothing waiting for her back in Argentina, but the shape and size of Dublin fits her like a cupped hand on a bare breast.

Ahead, Pavel stops and waits for the group to coalesce at the forking of the trail. In the distance, the summit of the hill rises like a tonsure through the trees.

———

A thin-skinned man with a tight, glowing forehead comes down the right-hand fork and steps to one side to let the four young people pass. His jeans are a darker blue all down one side from a sudden sideways attack of rain. The last of the group – a woman, he thinks, although her hair is cropped and her shoulders are as square as a boy's – turns back to wave at his dogs: a Malamute straining at a blue harness that disappears under a swaying sea of white foam, and a stocky Jack Russell with wedged shoulders and short legs.

The terrier is still nervous: two weeks ago, warning smudges of pink had appeared against the cream-coloured couch, but the man hadn't noticed and had left the dogs in the back garden together as usual. He had awoken to yelping and had seen the Malamute straddling the terrier from his upstairs window. Down the stairs, two by two, he had run outside with a hurley to whack at its thick white fur, but the dogs had been stuck by then, back to back, knotted together in a rush of bloody lust and panic. When they couldn't disengage, the Malamute had raced in circles around the garden, tugging the yelping terrier behind.

Two days later, the vet had tapped at a syringe full of dexamethasone and wrote down *abortifacient; mismating* in her daily case book. The Jack Russell had spent a full week panting and bleeding in equal measure, and the week after that her womb was removed. The stitches are only newly out and she is supposed to be on bedrest, but a wet, white panic had appeared around her eyes when he tried to sneak away for a walk without her.

She runs off-lead through the forest, now, looping figures of eight around the larger, leashed Malamute and detouring into the dense carpet of pine needles. She disappears to follow the scent of a rat, slipping into a thicket of brambles wrapped in twisting, heart-shaped leaves and splashes of white wood sorrel.

———

Ultan and Pavel discuss another cousin's elopement to Mexico as the terrier emerges from the trees, racing back down the trail to her owner. Their mothers are both distraught at the lack of a ceremony, but the lads are relieved that their suits can stay at the back of the wardrobe until the next family occasion; there were two weddings and four funerals last year in total.

how to gut a fish

Behind them, Elena tells Lauren that yesterday a hostel guest had tried to make tea in an electric kettle, and Lauren bends almost double in horrified hysterics. *Milk and all*, adds Elena and Lauren calls the boys back to tell them the story. *Milk and all*, Elena repeats, like an incantation.

On the distant hilltops, the history of logging is printed like braille. The stumps rise in graduated waves: moss grows wild on the oldest trunks and white, shrivelled logs record sharp dips below freezing point. But the day is mild and early damselflies flit around pockets of bog water; the unseasonably warm weather has caused the eggs to hatch too soon.

The forest path lifts, flattens, and rises again, between trees that are dark-needled and foreign; here and there, deep gashes are cut across the earth, bare-skinned stretches stubbled with char. Lauren makes detours, finding dappled patches of virgin soil to trace patterns with her boots. Yellow pine needles soon coat her legs up as far as her knees. Ultan tells her she looks like a wood-elf and she laughs, delighted, and pretends to aim an arrow at his heart.

A high wooden fort rises awkwardly above the trees. Stained timber sleepers encircle an acre of land that is greener than the rest of the forest, trimmed and sculpted into false hills and ditches. A white metal sign covered with colourful paint splatters whickers in the wind, welcoming birthday parties, team-building groups, hens and stags. At the bottom of the slope, three prefabs and a set of Portaloos are clustered. Heavy plastic firearms are hung on a wire, arranged into tribes by the blue or red of their feeder tubes. On the inside of the wooden fence, camouflaged bodysuits trail from metal hangers, waiting to be hosed down.

Through the slats, a teenage boy holding a power hose watches the four hikers pass by. A young woman with dark curls is laughing wildly at a man who is wielding a branch like a sword. The boy is jealous of their easy stride, the lightness of their passage; he finds his belly bulges more and more painfully against his waistband and he still has sweat stains under his armpits from the trek from the car park to the paintball arena. He kicks on the tap to spray down the bodysuits and the woman's laughter moves out of range through a rainbow mist.

The boy bites down on the back of his hand to stop a yawn; it is ticking towards lunchtime but he was up late playing a tactical death match with his friend in Warsaw. He had roared in frustration when he was shotgunned in the head and, from above, his father had slammed his closed fist twice into the floor of his bedroom. One bang could have been a falling book, and three would have been a message he could decipher, but just the two thuds made him afraid. His heart moved in his throat as he waited for the phrase to finish, for the chord to complete, and the silent, frozen moment stretched out until the thaw of dawn slipped under the garage door.

Now he has been sent to tidy up the staging area as his father has a large group from a broadband company booked in for Monday. There have been issues, the HR manager said in her email; issues in quotation marks, as if the problem is a self-contained unit that would be coming along on the trip to be exorcised, to be shot in the face with hard pellets of paint, to be stomped on and beaten to a bloody pulp in the waterlogged ditch between the wooden trellis and the junior play zone.

The boy wanders through the field with the hose, pointing it at areas of violence. The gelatine capsules usually dissolve in the rain but it has been a dryish February so far and the evidence of others that came before dispels the fantasy; takes the players out of the silver-screen mangroves of the Vietcong and back into a tree-shaved acre of artificial hills carved out of the Wicklow forest.

Against the drainage grate set in the centre of the concrete yard, a river of waxy colour swirls against itself, but the colours stay separate instead of merging into brown.

star jelly

Out of the shelter of the trees, the wind comes across the bare bogland horizontally, sheets of white that whip across the rain-slicked path; tight air that coils the lungs into knots and falls out again in steam.

At the final approach to the stone-pillared trig point, a blue sky unfolds itself and Pavel is the first to see the rocky cairn, precarious and ancient, but diminishing. Generations of hikers have secreted fossil souvenirs into their pockets to put on mantelpieces or discard on the car floor. The new custom — as detailed on a few hopeful signs erected by the tourist board — is to take a stone from the bottom of the hill and carry it to the top. The hikers haven't brought stones, but they have sandwiches from a roadside deli, filled with hard orange cheese and two-day-old lettuce, and they share lukewarm tea from Pavel's flask.

Lauren wanders off to match the grey slabs of the dolmen against a hazy memory of an image in her sixth-year art history workbook. Usually, on these day trips, she stores up artefacts and anecdotes to bring back for the hostel guests; every newcomer asks her advice on places to see. But her eyes are gritty from exhaustion and something drains out of her on the high and whistling summit, and she knows she will remember this morning only as a faint and distant dream.

Elena photographs the cairn's open mouth as her hill-sweat begins to cool against her skin. The clouds roll back in.

how to gut a fish

A woman in a purple puffer jacket sees the four figures moving over the stones at the summit and the small size of them makes her heart sink; there is still a long way to go. Her hiking boots are chafing; they are new and not yet broken in, and the leather heels are stiff against her Achilles tendons. Her little son is lagging behind, the tuft of his head just visible above a down-curve in the forest trail. His short legs are not the problem, more the fact that his head rotates constantly as if on a swivel, drinking in the green-yellows of the bog flowers, the powder grey of the granite, the royal purple of the sheaves of heather that begin as pinpricks but merge together into an endless carpet that coats the curve of the hill.

They won't go all the way to the summit, she decides; although there is a boardwalk that angles a path up the steep slope, the rain has made it slick-wet and, besides, her son would stop to look at every knothole, to poke his finger through the cage of chickenwire down to the rotting wood. She pushes on to the next bend and stops to let her ankles breathe, but the boy still doesn't notice her slipping away, still swivels his head from left, to down, to right, to down, as if unsure his legs will keep moving without his eyes to coax them on.

star jelly

There is a fierce knot of love in her for his eyes of a brown so sticky it catches in her teeth, but she wants to scream at him, tell him to *hurry to fuck*; that she didn't want to come in the first place; that the parking ticket is only good for two hours; that his small steps are multiplying the distance by two, four, eight and the hill will slope up and away forever, and they will be together, just the two of them, on an endless uphill trek.

She reaches into her backpack for a granola bar and breaks it cleanly down the middle, eats her half, and counts to one hundred as she waits for her son to close the distance between the two of them. The band of rage across her chest loosens as the sugar hits her bloodstream, and she moves off the boardwalk to allow the four silent hikers to pass her on their descent.

———

Halfway down the trail, Elena slips into the woods behind a fallen larch tree; wet clusters of tissue mark it as a common detour. Steaming urine splashes against the back of her calves and pools in the moss under her runners before sinking away, and she straightens to pull her leggings up over her hot, stinging thighs. And stops.

She calls to the others, and they do not hear her at first, arguing over whether to follow the red or yellow trail-blaze back down. Lauren is sure they took a left fork at this point, Ultan says the turn was to the right, even though he knows she is correct; her mock-annoyance as she slaps his shoulder leaves his entire skin tingling. Elena's call comes again, low and urgent, so they clamber over the waterlogged ditch and into the trees.

There is a clear jelly on the ground, a whitish mucous that has sprouted in an uneven pattern on a blanket of moss. It is thick and gloopy, wet between Ultan's outstretched fingers as Elena cautiously circles the clearing. *Frogspawn*, Lauren offers, but it's not the right season for it, he says, and anyway, this is all in one piece instead of small cells with single, inky dots. *Maybe some giants had an orgy*, suggests Pavel, dipping the toe of his steel-capped boot into one of the mounds and levering it into the air to splat against a tree trunk.

They are silent as they consider the possibilities. Perhaps the forest has recently sneezed, spewing wet lumps of snot out of its nostrils. Or it is some kind of mould, multiplying after a brief shower of warm rain; a life lived in fast-forward, ballooning outwards to die off again tomorrow. Or a frog, snapped up yesterday by a heron, and the black-tongued bird threw its head back in flight to retch up the swollen gonads, letting them fall down, down through the criss-crossing trees. Or the mess was deposited during the passing of a meteor, a shower of light and broken pieces of rock weeping across the sky, tearing itself to pieces under the weight of the atmosphere.

star jelly

The clouds clear suddenly, and stage lights dapple the clearing. Ultan kneels down on the carpet of moss to carefully photograph it on his phone; tapping the screen once, twice, three times; rotates the screen, zooms, and taps it again. He sniffs at the strange, radiant jelly, almost-tastes it, looks through it. It skewers the others into kaleidoscope pieces; five-sided shapes centred on a torso, a leg, an eye.

On the final descent into the car park, taking steep, juddering steps down the trail of oak sleepers, they stay silent, eyes watering in the sharpened wind. Lauren presses on ahead in exhaustion, cutting through the trees at a right angle to the zigzagging path. They fall away from each other and the distance between them stretches until their grouping breaks, and they are, each one, walking alone.

Ultan, trailing at the back and floating from lack of sleep, stops to check his phone and finds a sweet pocket of stillness. Around him, Sitka trees whipper in the wind; a rivulet of rain cracks the grey limestone. A smudge of a wide-winged bird crosses the sky and his runners scrape against the crisp stone. In the silence, his head seems to unfold from an origami knot and flatten out into a clean, white sheet of paper.

how to gut a fish

The residue of the strange jelly has dried on his fingers. He rubs his hands together and raises them to his face, but they smell of nothing at all.

A white flash, and a terrier barrels around a bend, chased by a pale shock of a bald man who is hauling on a second dog's harness to stop his gape-mouthed lope. They pass, and Ultan searches for the indentation of quiet again, but a siren begins and flattens into a child's knee-skint keen, coming from further up the trail. He stretches and yawns, rolling his head around in a clicking circle, and the bones in his thighs begin the dull, metallic ache of tiredness. The sky is white again, down on the lowlands, beneath the weaving of clouds. Across the treetops, a Jolly Roger flag lashes the wind above the high walls of a fort, but Ultan squints and he can see that it is the darkest blue instead of black.

———

The girls are leaning on the car when he reaches the end of the trail; Pavel rolls a cigarette between cold, clumsy fingers and dives for the lighter as soon as the door is unlocked. Ultan's eyes close when he hits the baked warmth of the car and a thumping begins behind his left eye. His throat feels scratched from his friend's unfamiliar packet of Arabic-lettered tobacco, and he swallows twice to ease some phlegm over the rawness. He opens his eyes again and sees that his tax disc is almost out of date; he must remember to take a thick black marker and change the number; to force time on by a year.

The sun is directly in his eyes as he pulls on to the corkscrew road. He lowers the flap to partially block the spears of light and sees in the rear mirror that Lauren has her eyes closed, but she isn't asleep; her chin is raised so high he can see the horseshoe shape of her jaw, the fresh spring sunlight catching in the down of her dark chin, the thumb-smears in the mirror encasing her face in a translucent gel.

He decides he will take a roundabout way home, dropping Pavel off first and leaving Lauren to last. When she shakes herself awake to get out of his car, he will ask for her phone number, to send her the photos of the star jelly, to continue the gentle argument, shore up the fragile connection.

Her pupils tremble under her lids and he realises he is staring. He turns back to the grass-bellied road and drops his window to let cold air stream across his forehead, but her face, her glowing, horseshoe face, grows and changes in the mirror; the angles and hues are translated into other languages; into numbers and shapes and smells; into the feeling of the steering wheel under his thick and warming fingers.

dome

Warm morning light trickles in from the apex and is reflected off buildings and red metal seamarks, stabbing at the deep dark of the ocean. Some batters its way down past the foam rollers, weakens and resurfaces; blue sheens into green-black and back again to white. A salted film of wave rolls up and over to split white across a knife-curl and rejoin itself, hold, and break apart again.

On the next plane down, hundreds of fish fry spool like metal filings, following underwater leylines, stopping to spin solemn circles and conductor-flick off at angles, converging again into a whole. Down, down under the sand, the razor clams burrow with a pale muscle, a tongue stretched to its thickest in a mouth full of secrets.

Sea meets land at the spume of high water. Spaghetti squiggles of soil on a rippled, finger-waved beach. Clumpings of grass and noise make uneven rows of sand dunes, eaten away by the flood of spring tides. At the end of the beach, a stretched bar of sand reaches out into the ocean and curves around into a spiral, protecting the pier from the worst of the storms.

A rocky breakwall and promenade separate the marram grass from the last outposts of the village: the whickering of a newsagent's shutter, a paint-peeling café, a darkened chip shop, a glass-fronted notice-board. Dew glistens off a squatting line of rental bikes and blood-beaked gulls ride updraughts above a semi-circle of houses. Two early-morning buses bustle by, and the streetlights blink off. Tilt up, and the leftover moon is a button on the dome of a blue anorak.

The early dippers are skin-bagged around the hips and come with rosebud towels for their summer swim, strapping their heads down with bright silicone. The women – one man came before, in shrink-wrapped swim shorts, but a clot has left him in a shaded hospice room – clasp hands with their eyes from opposite sides of the pier and descend the stone steps, slapping at prickling skin, forcing themselves into the sea.

The women are a tower of dents, and their hurts need daily poulticing with ice-cold saltwater. Most are hairline fissures, but others have been driven in with chisels: the silent closure of a door, the sound of an open slap on skin, the thud of raspberries against the earth and pink-beaked blackbirds flying away.

The frigid surface of the sea splits the world into before and after; between them comes the now – the chest tightening, the panting, the stunning of the cold. The women pause, to find their own reasons why again, and move on, shoulders frittering for warmth. The morning light on the clear water bends their legs into faint, following wraiths.

Morning dog walkers point the swimmers out to each other and shiver to themselves as the women breaststroke their way to the lollipop buoys and back.

The tired curve of the moon dips below the buildings and first warmth begins to percolate from the ceiling of summer clouds. An eye-bright sky.

A double-decker bus pulls in at the car park on the hill and a group of tourists unfolds itself, already clicking their cameras. The tour guide gestures to the sea tower and they pick their way forward on to the grassy cliff edge, around empty beer cans and plastic forks.

A blue rope dangles from the tower window at head-height, knotted around fists of wood. A man with a bare belly levers himself against the stone wall, arching his back; he falls awkwardly to the ground on ankles untempered by the bus journey and rubs the burn of the rope away on his trouser legs.

how to gut a fish

The rest of the group billows out along the cliffs in a cloud that cools and converges again around the official red uniform. A literary lesson by the snot-green sea, and the Polish tour guide fields questions: *where are you really from?*

Afterwards, the tourists break to flatten themselves against the landscape and browse the morning markets. They buy spoons carved from bogwood, resin-cast fridge magnets, freshly baked bread. A puffer-pink woman buys day-old, unshucked oysters from a pile of ice; her hotel has a mini-fridge, hopefully.

The sun comes out in mid-morning, and the low water is as warm as an hour-old bath.

A blue, high-shouldered van spills out kayaks on to a slipway. Buoyancy aids pile up, red and sweating, rimmed with white tide marks. The kayaking instructor has done three trips out into the bay already this weekend, and the salt itches in his psoriasis-scaled armpits. He tightens foot straps and measures the waiting clients with his eyes, finding the natural pairs for the double-handed canoes. Two and two and two, and one leftover. The hopeful group have vouchers with no expiry date, the promise of flat waves and possibly a seal sighting. *It's something different*, they nod at each other, *something to do*; they grasp at Sunday-morning wellness in the warming air.

Hangovers throb with shame and a sweet staleness rises into a haze as all seven struggle into still-damp wetsuits, nervously rubbing at jutting bellies and bared ankles, testing the chafe of neoprene.

A safety briefing from the instructor, a demonstration, their phones are slotted into waterproof slips. The heavier, broad-nosed canoes take two handlers each, one at the front and one at the back; the plastic stern of the single-hander leaves a V-shaped drag mark in the sand.

The boats launch in the shallow water, and the instructor backpaddles his streamlined, white-water kayak out beyond the surf. The training canoes wallow and spill over; a woman lets out a shriek as the water reaches her groin.

Finally settled, their paddles smack against the surface, find an awkward rhythm, and the fleet moves off against the quickening sea breeze, coaxed out by the gentle sun.

The tide hums to itself and turns over in thought.

A four-limbed aerial drone buzzes above the promenade, turning sharp corners like a fruit fly, invisible hands directing it from the car park. The machine sets out over the water, confident, breaking for the horizon. A few metres further, it reaches the edge of its operating range and begins to stutter, falling in stop-motion before it comes back under the owner's panicked control and boomerangs in towards shore.

A teeth-edged whine rises over the beach as the drone grows closer to its remote controller. A father looks up from the headlines on his tablet to shield his young daughter's face from the machine; he has read about airborne cameras taking illicit photographs in the red-top newspapers.

The girl digs with a flattened spade, channelling a dug-pool of water to the sea, rainbow-strapped togs biting into her dark, gently sloping back. She has made a throne for the hollowed-out carcass of a crab and decorated it with dried seaweed.

Limpets in rockpools scrape against bare knees where sawn-off wetsuits end. Two brown-haired boys find a star-centred jellyfish stranded by the tide and pull it to pieces with sticks; the stinging cells are toothless against their water-safe sandals.

Their words have soft edges and blend into a solemn discussion about hermit crabs. One boy says the shell is a house, and houses get smaller as you grow; his

chafes at the shoulders already. The younger thinks
a shell grows in place, like toenails. He once crushed
a snail on a darkened doorstep and made a lunchbox hospital with dock leaves and a capful of water;
in the morning, the death-foam and yellow splits of
the snail's intestines had made him lick his fingers in
fright.

The boys' mothers sun themselves on a slab of
concrete at the top of the beach; one in a crimson
one-piece that spills out twin tufts of dark pubic hair
against stretch-marked thighs, the other in a faded,
flowering blouse and high denim shorts.

They discuss a minor scandal in the local primary
school, find holes to poke in the weavings of commit-
tees. One-piece stands to curve her spine around,
fingers splayed on each side of her leather sandals,
then rummages in a towel-swollen knapsack for a
lunchtime snack of crackers, sliced vegetables and
rounded cheeses.

Her friend shifts on the hard concrete, uncomfort-
able, the unbroken spine of a book at her feet. The fat
has fallen away from her pelvis, leaving her balanced
on bony stilts, and the thick, black spouts of hair at the
other woman's groin have annoyed her.

A sand dune away from them, the two boys are
arguing over a heated transaction of shells. Spiralling
periwinkles are coppers, empty razor clams are silver,
and the single, almost-whole sea urchin is gold.

how to gut a fish

The tide is climbing against the cliff face again.

Afternoon, and a fat set of speakers pants out heavy, dustbin beats. Teenage skin throbs against waistbands as the boys trickle down the path to the overhang. They sweat and tease and shout over each other: in their mouths, lyrics are dissected, mothers fuck and are fucked, teachers face imaginary shotguns. Greasy chips sweat against brown paper bags, vinegar stings in nervously torn cuticles.

A sign pleads NO DIVING, an arched black figure barred by a red line, because necks have been broken here, come out of the ocean in a shoulder-flop, eyes blank under dipped eyelids. But the jump is the thing, not the before or after.

The first boy approaches the edge casually, but his anxious feet scuff against tufts of grass. Eyes meet the horizon and the arms begin to whir, knees lock as the speed increases, faster! the cupping of the rock falls away and the air is treacle in a five-second freefall. A blast of an entry; the water recovers and the surface is broken again by fine, strawberry hair plastered against a wet skull.

The other boys wait their turn, tossing insults over and back like heated coals. A single cigarette is shared out among them; the one asthmatic boy wanders away in embarrassment to look at the seashell jewellery stall.

dome

A brief evening squall blows in over the outer light-house, lifting the air and tossing it like a stained mattress. Concrete wetly darkens and the warm sky sighs down.

Out in the bay, a paint-stripped chugger pulls lobster pots up and against the gunnels. The cages are empty; the skipper pauses, and the boat turns into the wind.

Further out, a larger boat with a cabin slides past, the heavy smell of rotten fish ground into the metal decking. A stag party flings mackerel guts at the wind, and purple trickles down their wrists. They shiver over beers that share a cooler with the ungutted carcass of a prized turbot.

On the next orbit out, a ferry crosses, built from blocks and scaled with windows. The three boats meet each other in a cutting-out and a melding of silhouettes, then split again and move apart. The chugger is left alone to return to the shore, where the high tide has swallowed the ladder rungs and the fenders float at the pier's lip.

The rolling swell from the ferry comes a little later, almost breaching the sea wall.

The gloaming blankets down and the tide drains away. A stop-motion sky darkens in gradients and the temperature begins to drop in uneven mouth-fuls. Shutters fall and the few remaining market stalls are draped in white sheets; leftover bread spirals are doled out by the Finnish baker, rye-dark and heavy as a bezoar.

The single, low-ceilinged pub fills halfway and the thump of music travels out towards the mountains in the still air. It is two for one on Sex on the Beach cocktails, and the DJ has brought his good decks along for the occasion.

At midnight, the crowd empties from the pub to brighten the chip shop, smash half-empty pint glasses and shriek laughter at the sky. The last buses whistle by.

Two dogs bicker from opposite sides of the darkened pier, one short-pitched and shrill, the other deep and lowing; an old argument of evenings. Night settles in, creaking and plinking.

A grey, scraped hatchback parks diagonally across the white lines in the car park. The fluorescent, blood-orange glow from the streetlamps squeaks against the glass and runs down in rivulets. Smoke lazes from a half-raised window, and cigarette ash piles into gunpowder. Fingers trace knuckles, so softly that shivers run from ear to ear, spiralling. Voices arpeggio up; words come out half-formed and taste of wanting and witness.

The hatchback pulls out again on to the low sea road.

dome

The stars are clouded in gossamer.

The night catches and pools in the swirl of the newsagent's plastic ice-cream cone; the curve of a man's inner ear as he sleeps in an alcoved doorway; the extending arm of the swept-away beach.

The land sits in place and beats against a circle of horizons, moving further from the sun. Tow-lines run out from the cliff's jagged edge to the domed, navy sky, needle-pricked with stars, a hundred, thousand points of light, dragging it closer, faster and faster.

All things fall inward, and the last clouds slip away.

The sky, the sky.

Acknowledgements

Thanks to my parents, Máire and Bryan, for humouring me. You are the reason I was able to write this book and anything at all. Thanks to Frances, Aileen, Peter and Beth. I am so lucky to have four wise siblings to go to for advice. My nieces Cleo, Stella, Laura and Kate, and nephew Nicky, for being the brightest part of my day. Thanks also to the extended Armstrong and Maye families for endless support, and to Peter and cousin Frank for fact-checking how to *actually* gut a fish. In memory, also, of my late uncle Francis, who would have been delighted to tell me what I got wrong.

To editors Dave Lordan and Susan Tomaselli, who took an early punt on me when I didn't know what I was doing (I still don't, but I hide it better). To my writing group, Chekhov or Fuck off, who I met on the *Stinging Fly*'s excellent six-month workshop. They read early drafts of everything and explained to me what I was on about. So many times, a stray comment or suggestion from them has pivoted a story around entirely – if there's a good idea in

Acknowledgements

here it probably came from there. To Cill Rialaig hags and Gin Misfits, for lockdown solidarity and general literary troubleshooting. Thanks also to the Irish Writers' Centre and the Stinging Fly for their courses and support.

To my agent, Marianne Gunn O'Connor, for kindly ignoring my protests and believing in me instead. Dan Bolger, for his early interest in my stories and excellent edits.

To Catherine, Deirdre, Sarah, everyone past and present at Gill Books; Maeve, Sarah and Stephanie. When I left my editorial job to write this book, you didn't laugh and instead gave me excellent advice about sitting on this side of the table.

To Paul Baggaley and Charlotte Greig, Sara Helen Binney, Sarah-Jane Forder, Charlotte Norman, Joel Arcanjo, Jonathon Leech, David Mann, Amy Donegan, Ros Ellis and everyone at Bloomsbury – I know how the sausage is made, and it's not easy. Thank you for making the shaping, production and packaging process so smooth (I'll change the metaphor now in case it gets out of control).

To Jonny, Killian and Kyle – woo-hoo! Who would have guessed reading and writing would pay off. Apparently, you don't win friends with salad, so it must have been an excellent recipe to win me you three eejits. Dee, Jess, Susan, Sinead, Aisling, Marian, Eimear, Helen, Maebh, Darcy, Gemma, Lisa, Jacinta

Acknowledgements

and all the UCS girls – vote me *second* most likely to write a book? The cheek. Roísín & Phil (plus two!), Laura, Kevin, Langan and all the Sligo heads, for beer, boats and mountain baps.

Thanks to Paul. Now get out of my office. No, I don't need anything. Get out, Paul.

Most of all, to everyone whose life I rifled through and stole details, images, conversations and ideas. I once saw a trained racoon pickpocketing food out of people's trouser pockets. It didn't apologise, but I do – and thank you.

A Note on the Author

Sheila Armstrong is a writer and editor from the north-west of Ireland. This is her first book of fiction.

A Note on the Type

The text of this book is set in Bembo, which was first used in 1495 by the Venetian printer Aldus Manutius for Cardinal Bembo's *De Aetna*. The original types were cut for Manutius by Francesco Griffo. Bembo was one of the types used by Claude Garamond (1480–1561) as a model for his Romain de l'Université, and so it was a forerunner of what became the standard European type for the following two centuries. Its modern form follows the original types and was designed for Monotype in 1929.